Concrete Jungle

By: Naheem

First print 2017 June

This is a book of fiction. Any references or similarities to actual events, real people, or real locations are intended to give the novel a sense of reality. Any similarity to other names, characters, places and incidents are entirely coincidental.

ISBN-13:978-1978478411
ISBN-10:1978478410

Cover Design: Dynasty

Book Productions: Crystell Publications
You're The Publisher, We're Your Legs
We Help You Self Publish Your Book
(405) 414-3991

Every Saint has a past… Every Sinner has a future!

-Author Unknown

DEDICATION

Concrete Jungle is dedicated to my Mother, Gwen Fenwick (R.I.P) & My Son, Prince Naheem Robert Fenwick.

ACKNOWLEDGMENTS

First and foremost I give thanks to Allah (SWT), The Most Kind and The Most Merciful, for it is He (SWT)who illuminates my path.

I want to thank the two leading ladies in my life, my grandmothers. (Thanks for ya'll love and support). I also would like to thank the rest of my family for the inspiration and motivation they've been throughout the years. I would also like to thank my typist Anthony Burns AKA Musa. Last but not least, I want to thank my staff at Media 44 and everyone over at All We Got Iz Us Publications.

R.I.P.

Robert "Black Rob" Tyson, Lil'Anthony, White Boy Tony, Adam Fenwick, Big Yvette, Gil, Lil'Charles, Colin, Lil'Maine Mitter, Troy, Charles "Pop Bottlez" Mitter, Pooch, Rose, Tay-Bo, Drip, Kapo, Meaty, Sly, Donte.

If I failed to mention anyone, I might've forgot about you, like you forgot about me!!!

PROLOGUE

Lord know I know, I feel like can't nobody fuck with me, And God got my back so, Boosie keep his mind at ease.

Lil Boosie's powerful lyrics followed by heavy 808's and intricate drum patterns roared through the Bose speakers as Naheem maneuvered in and out of the flow of traffic at 88mph on Interstate 395. Fighting to keep his eyes open, Naheem was determined to live as he tried to regulate his breathing. He was hit pretty bad. His injuries included a shot to the left bicep and one to the left calf muscle, both of which were in and out wounds. More concerned with the wound in his abdomen, he removed his hand from the burning wound against his gut and noticed he was bleeding profusely.

As Naheem passed the Raven's M&T stadium he glanced at his almost useless blood drenched hand and at that very moment he felt a chill over his body although beads of perspiration burst through his pores like a linebacker through an offensive line. Naheem shifted his gaze from his hand back to the wound in his stomach. The hole was no bigger than that of a pencil. The bottom half of Naheem's white Affliction shirt was dark red. Placing his hand back over the wound Naheem thought out loud and shook his head from side to side.

"Shit! Bitch ass niggaz got me good."

Visions of Netta and Prince quickly flooded him, forcing him into overdrive. At the thought of possibly dying and leaving his son another tear managed to escape his right eye.

"Gotta get to the hospital."

Feeling his heavy eyelids attempting to close, Naheem snapped back to reality and willed himself to stay alert. On the lookout for the police, every so often he peeked up into his rearview mirror to scan the traffic behind him. Finally, after weaving around several cars to get ahead, he pressed his foot all the way down on the gas pedal and the car shot up to 110 mph and pinned him back against his seat.

Bearing to the right on the Hanover Street exit, Naheem decided it would be best if he slowed down to a moderate speed to approach the light. After crossing the Hanover Street bridge Naheem thought, "Damn, the hospital only up the street."

The hospital that he had in mind was Harbor Hospital which was now approximately three hundred yards ahead. Naheem was ten feet from the last light he had to go through to make the left in the hospital's parking lot when he lost consciousness and went through the red light. The huge loss of blood sent Naheem into shock causing him to lose consciousness again. His state of comatose was so deep that as he rolled through the red light he wasn't even awaken when a speeding F-150 ran into the passenger side of his car in the middle of the intersection spinning it over forty-five degrees. The car veered off to the left and came down on all four wheels when it hit the curb. With the hospital only a hundred yards ahead Naheem lay slumped in his car motionless dangling helplessly between life and death.

The airbags in the F-150 exploded on impact temporarily knocking the woman and her girlfriend out. The two young women awake moments later to several pedestrians trying to pry their doors open. Due to impact, both doors were jammed. The young ladies climbed out the driver side window. With tears in her eyes and her right hand over her mouth the driver managed to say, "OO-MMY-GAWD!"

She saw the horrific sight of a man laid on the sidewalk with so much blood on him, nobody could place its source. The man lay on little pieces of broken windshield glass that the sun reflected off, causing the street and sidewalk to look as if diamonds had grown from the concrete. The F-150's driver broke down into heavy sobs while her girlfriend held her in a comforting manner. Her sobs were so loud that she didn't hear the spectator that tried to take Naheem's pulse.

"You can stick a fork in this one baby, he done."

The passenger of the F-150 comforted her girlfriend as tears rolled silently down her face.

CHAPTER 1

Sitting in his $1,700 a month condo in the Owings Mills section of Maryland called New Town, Naheem sat quietly on the edge of his California King bed which served as the place of rest for him and the love of his life Netta who for the moment was asleep. As Naheem sat on the side of the bed half dressed in only a light blue pair of Robin's jeans, he begun to slip on his black and grey Prada shoes. The soft sultry sounds of Anita Bakers voice could be heard coming from the hidden speakers of the surround sound Bose system that was moderate in volume but seemed to make passionate love to anyone ear that cared to listen.

At twenty two years of age, Naheem had been in the streets since he was 12. His mother died of H.I.V, she'd caught a bad case of bronchitis that her immune system was too weak to fight off. He'd seen and been through a lot at a young age on the uncaring streets of Baltimore which caused him to develop a hard cold glare in his eyes. The fact of the matter was, all his trials and tribulations caused him to have an old soul.

This day wasn't any different from any other but

Naheem was still thankful for his current position in life. Just as he finished tying his shoe, Naheems three year old son Prince ran in the room and jumped into his father's arms. The speed that he amassed along with his solid 65 pound frame caused Naheem to lay back on the bed with Prince now sitting on his chest.

"You act like you miss me," Naheem shot at the pint size version of himself.

Prince countered not giving thought to his father's statement.

"I hungry Da-Da."

"I just bet you are big boy, what you wanna eat?"

"Candy!"

"Naw big boy, I'll get you some candy later. How about some cheese eggs?"

Prince sat for a second as if he was pondering the elements of gravity then said, "and fros flake too Da- Da?"

Smiling at the mispronunciation of the cereal and Prince's huge appetite, Naheem chuckled and said, "Yeah... And fros flake too."

"Okay Da-Da." Prince said climbing down from his father's chest.

"Go wait for me in the living room while I get ready."

Without a reply young Prince was gone just as fast as he came. Coming from the walk in closet with a white V-neck T-shirt in hand, Naheem noticed Netta staring up at him from the comfort of the thousand count thread sheets that covered her naked body up to her neck. With a soft smile on his face Naheem began with, "Good morning Cupcake."

Netta smiled back and jokingly retort, "That boy getting

so damn big he gonna have to get a job soon."

"That's my little football player right there." Naheem responded as he pulled the T-shirt over his head.

Netta was 5 feet 10 inches tall with neatly spaced locks that fell inches below her shoulders. At 165 pounds she sported a 35-27-41 frame that most video models would pay for but she was all natural. Although she had a body to kill for, it was her dark sun kiss complexion that drove Naheem over the top. Besides Netta's complexion, Naheem thought her best asset was her loyalty to him. She wasn't Prince's mother but she looked at him as her son.

When Prince was seven months old his mother dropped him off at Naheem's grandmother house never to be seen or heard from again. Word on the street was Prince's mother was strung out on heroin and was prostituting to feed her habit.

"I'm hungry too daddy." Netta said with lust in her eyes as she waited for her man to respond.

Knowing what she was hinting around to Naheem said, "You ain't get enough last night?"

"Ima big girl with a big appetite."

"I see... I can't play right now I got a few things to do and a grown ass man to feed." Naheem told her as he playfully jumped on the huge bed beside her.

Although she understood she was still a little disappointed, she just couldn't get enough of the man she'd grown to love.

"Well, I guess I'll get in the shower then."

Naheem kissed her on the forehead while raising himself up off the bed. He headed for the door and stopped.

"You want some fros flakes."

As if on cue Netta shot back in a lustful voice with all pun intended, "I told you, Ima big girl I need meat!"

For a split second Naheem started to take her up on her offer but he thought better of it. As Naheem walked out the room he turned to Netta who was now sitting up in bed.

"I love you Cupcake."

"I love you more." Were the words that he heard as he crossed the threshold and shut the bedroom door.

Prince sat in the living room watching cartoons on TV, the living room was adjacent to the kitchen where his father prepared breakfast for them. By the time Prince and Naheem had finished eating Netta was walking out the bedroom into the kitchen fresh out the shower in a thick white terrycloth robe with her locks neatly wrapped in a towel.

"What y'all doin today?" Naheem asked.

"Me and Prince gonna go to the aquarium, you know the Lion King came back out in 3D so we gonna catch that then I guess I'll take him to your grandmother's house. He told me he wanna see his Na-Na."

"I see Na-Na Da-Da!"

Naheem smiled at his son and told him, "That's what's up. You got a big day planned."

Netta continued, "We should be in by 8:30 no later than 9."

"You need anything!" Naheem asked now standing and facing Netta.

"No, I'm good."

Disregarding what he'd just been told, Naheem removed

two one hundred dollar bills from a nice size wad of cash that he had in his right pocket. Placing the bills in front of Netta she snapped.

“I told you, I'm good!”

“Take the money or I'll rip it!” Naheem said with conviction.

For a brief second Netta just looked at the bills then Naheem bent down and gave them to Prince.

“Here you go little man, have fun.”

“Net look, Da-Da give me money!”

Netta smiled at the way Naheem spoils her and Prince.

“I see, let me put it up for you so you don't lose it.”

Prince handed her the bills and asked, “I rich now Net?”

“Not yet but almost.”

Naheem grabbed Netta by her waist just as she was removing her hand from the pocket of her robe where she tucked the bills. He pulled her close to him and passionately kissed her. Their tongues danced and twirled like snakes doing a mating dance. Naheem broke the rhythm of the heated kiss by slowly backing away as he lightly sucked on her bottom lip.

“I love you Cupcake.”

“I love you more baby,” Netta said feeling herself getting moist. Naheem turned to Prince and proceeded with his good-byes.

“Awight shorty, Ima see you later. Tell Na-Na I love her.”

“Love you Da-Da,” Prince said hugging his father.

“I love you too Big Head.”

Soon Naheem was out and headed to his black 2007 S55

Mercedes Benz. He sat in the comfort of the cars leather interior. The pressing of the ignition button brought it to life as Naheem reached in his armrest to remove his other phone. Checking his "Bitch Box" as he call it, Naheem scrolled through the phone checking for unanswered calls and text messages. He pressed a button opening the sunroof and noticed the sky was clear. At 60° degrees 9:25 in the morning it was sure to be a good day.

Naheem turned the CD player to disk 6. He pressed four buttons at the same time and brought all four windows of the car down. Naheem turned a knob raising the volume and rapped along with the rapper feeling his energy.

Ima full time hustler,
I'm full time real,
A full time D-boy,
I get it how I live,
I full time grind,
So I full time shine,
And I'm full time strapped,
With a fully loaded nine...

With that, Naheem pulled out of the parking garage on his way to East Baltimore.

CHAPTER 2

Usually Naheem would've taken the highway to get to the eastside of Baltimore but today he decided he would drive into the city the long way. As Liberty Rd. turned into Liberty Heights the traffic began to thicken. Once on the west side Naheem saw young hustlers setting up their drug shops for what many of them hoped would be a profitable day. Naheem smiled in acknowledgement at the ambition of the young hustlers as he drove through the concrete jungle.

Naheem continued down Pennsylvania Ave. until he got to the busy intersection of North Ave. where everything seemed to be moving faster. Crowds of people rushed to and from the escalator which sat directly on the corner. The escalator lead to the subway underground. Above ground on the opposite side of the street angry men and women appeared to be waiting for the building they stood in front of to open. That building was a free clinic.

On the other side of the street from the clinic were touters who stood along the store fronts advertising different brands of heroin shouting names like Red Dot, X-

Box, White Diamond and Kush. Naheem made a left onto North Ave. when his phone began to vibrate. He looked at the screen and it read 887 which was his man Nasir's code.

"What it do?"

"You already know my nig, just laxin waitin on you."

"That's what's up. I'm on North now, I'll be there in a minute."

"I can dig it. I'll holla when you get here."

"That's what it is."

The line was disconnected and the phone was placed back in its holster. Nasir had been nothing short of loyal to Naheem. Their bond was unbreakable and Naheem saw that Nasir was worthy of being in his inner circle. He did everything he could to help Nasir from putting him in a townhome in Glen Burnie Maryland to giving him the job of being his top lieutenant which meant that Nasir ran all of the drug shops. Every morning Nasir and Naheem met at an apartment they called the safehouse to discuss the progress of the day before and to lay the plans of any future business. Nasir would bring the proceeds from the Brooklyn Park, Streeper Street and Aiken Street shops and the cash would be divvied.

The safehouse complex was located in the quiet Northeast section of Baltimore directly on the corners of LochRaven and the Alameda. Naheem turned the volume down as he pulled into the parking lot of the nice size complex. He drove past the building of his destination all the way to the end of the parking lot by a huge green dumpster. Naheem was now five apartment buildings from his intended destination. He closed the sunroof and rolled the windows up while checking his surroundings then stepped out the car and headed towards the safehouse.

Once at the front door of the apartment building Naheem noticed Nasir's burgundy Range Rover parked three cars up. As he punched in a code on the key pad the door made a clicking sound and Naheem was in the building on his way to the third floor. Inside the apartment Nasir and Naheem gave each other some dap and sat on a black leather sofa in front of a little glass table with three piles of money on it.

Overall, the safehouse appeared to be a regular apartment with its soft black leather loveseat and lounge chair that served as the living room with a circular crystal table that sat on a chrome hourglass base. A 64 inch flat screen sat diagonally in the right hand corner along with an entertainment system that consisted of a DVD player, subwoofer and four surround sound speakers. Beside the entertainment system was a five foot tall DVD rack. All the kitchen cabinets were empty with the exception of one that was stocked with plastic cups and paper plates while a bag of plastic forks sat on the counter top. Both bedrooms were empty with the exception of their neatly made beds. The bathroom was basic other than the safe that was tucked away under the sink in its cabinet.

Nasir got straight to the point and reached down to the table to push one pile of money over in front of Naheem.

“This fifteen came from Aiken. It's really startin to pick up down there. Tye and his lil men doin their thing.”

Naheem counted the fifteen thousand dollars then thought for a brief second before he spoke.

"Okay... Take Tye off salary and give him thirty percent off everything they move. He'll see his money every day so he can pay the shop on a salary once a week."

With a look of confusion on his face Nasir said, "Hold up, you talkin too fast."

Naheem counted the last of the fifteen thousand and countered.

"Naw nigga, I ain't talkin fast you listenin slow. Tye pulled in fifteen last night right?"

"Yeah."

"Now we gon start givin him twenty... he'll give us fourteen and keep six stacks a day for himself and he'll pay the hitters, lockouts, touters and the rest of the shop out of that. In the end he should have at least twenty five for himself."

"Yeah, that's a good look for shorty," Nasir said as he shoved the smaller pile of neatly stacked money in front of Naheem.

"This came out of Brooklyn, Dutch say it's slow."

"What's goin on down there?" Naheem questioned.

"Shorty say all kinds of D.T.'s and jump outs comin through since the lil stickup nigga ShyBorn got hit."

"Oh yeah... somebody caught that cruddy lil bitch huh," Naheem asserted with a slight grin on his face.

"Hell yeah." Nasir continued, "Two to the face. They said the lil dirty bitch Kandie was out there screamin and cryin, talkin about he ain't dead don't cover him up and a few of his dreads was layin a few feet away from the body."

"Good damn job well done. Call Lou and Howie,

tell'em thanks for the favor." Nasir changed the subject.

"They only pulled in seven, it shouldn't stay hot down there. I'll give it another week before shit back clickin again."

"Free throws and fouls, it's all in the game," Naheem said knowing the drug game was as predictable as the wind.

After counting the seven thousand dollars it was placed on the far end of the table with money previously counted. Nasir didn't bother to move the remaining sum of cash, he just slightly nodded his head towards it and spoke.

"That's twenty six that come off the block."

The block that Nasir spoke of was Streeper Street. Naheem took pride in Streeper, that was the block that he'd built with his own blood, sweat and tears. Streeper was the start of it all, Naheem could remember being on that block going hand to hand when it only produced barely five hundred dollars a day. Days like today make it all worth it he thought to himself. Now Streeper was a top earner. Naheem heard Nasir say, "Nephew doin his thing, shorty know how to run a block."

At 14 years of age five feet four inches and weighing 130 pounds, Nephew ran Streeper with an iron fist. His babyface was a far cry from the ferociousness engraved in his heart. Nephew had known Naheem most of his life from growing up on Streeper. His mother was addicted to heroin and overdosed when he was eight. Coming in from school one day, Nephew walked in the house to the kitchen only to find his mother laid out on the floor eyes wide open and needle still in her arm. Unfazed by the tragic sight, Nephew turned and calmly walked outside and found Naheem. At eight years old and with a look in his eyes as if he witnessed all of life's misfortunes Nephew looked up at Naheem and spoke.

"My mother OD'd yo."

From that day on Naheem looked at Nephew like his own showing him the ropes and teaching him how to pull his own weight in the streets.

Naheem snapped out of his thoughts of the past to deal with the business at hand. He told Nasir, "Yeah, shorty came a long way. I been thinkin about givin you and Nephew the game. You can deal straight with Roberto yourself and Nephew can be your right hand man."

With a chuckle Nasir blurt out, "You been thinkin this shit or Netta been thinkin it for you?"

"Both," came his answer with a boyish grin.

The two men broke out in laughter when Naeem's phone vibrated. He screened the call and saw 00020.

"What it do my nig?"

"You already fuckin know G. " Came Kayo's response.

Excited to hear his friends voice Kayo continued, "I start trial Monday yo."

"That's what it is, call me when the shit over."

"Awight... yo, I got a new chick tryna move, you might remember her. She use to work K section when you was over here."

"What's her name?"

"Ms. Brockington, Sherry Brockington."

"Oh yeah, I do remember her."

"Look yo, give her an ounce of loud, a carton of cigarettes and five hundred. I'll have the shit the next day."

"Awight, give her my number."

“That's what it is, don't try to fuck my bitch yo.” Kayo said jokingly.

“I don't want that bitch, I want the last little chick you had, what was her name uuhhh.. Stokes, yeah that's it.”

“You talkin about Ciara. Maaan, she quit a few months ago. She said she was goin back to school.”

Kayo changed the subject, “Yo, guess who my cell buddy is?”

“Who?” Naheem asked with curiosity in his voice.

“Vailz!”

“Man put that nigga on the phone.”

“Suga Da Pimp speaking.” Vialz said.

“Yo, why the fuck you ain't been getting at me? I was blowin your phone up.”

“When I was on J section, one of those hate‘in niggaz dropped a note on me and got me shook down. When Rasco found my phone I got 30 days on the hammer.” Vialz said still sounding a bit frustrated about the correctional officers taking his phone.

“Look.. Dig this, tell Kayo Ima give the Brockington broad a stack and another horn for you.”

“Good lookin out my nig,” Vialz answered.

“When you comin…”

Naheem was cut off in mid-sentence when Vialz rambled through his next set of words.

“It's count time, Rasco on the move, we’ll holla later.”

The line was disconnected. Back at the Maryland Correctional Detention Center Kayo hurriedly took down the sheet that hung on the bars in front of the cell that gave them privacy. Vialz handed Kayo back the phone and in return Kayo gave Vialz the phones charger. Both of them tucked the contents into the crotch pockets of their boxer brief underwear.

In the safe house, Nasir spoke first.

"Who was that, Kayo?"

"Yeah," Naheem responded as he counted out 11 thousand of the twenty six. Leaving the other fifteen thousand in its place Naheem gestured to it.

"That's you right there."

Nasir took the money and nonchalantly walked to the kitchen where he placed the money in an empty drawer. Meanwhile Naheem scooped the thirty three thousand and started towards the bathroom. Once in the bathroom he bent down and opened the cabinet under the sink exposing an electronic safe with a key pad which look much like that of a phone. When Naheem began punching in numbers on the key pad red lights came to life on its screen. Every time he pushed a number a red * would appear on the safe's small screen. When the last digit was punched in, the red lights danced around on the screen before they formed the word OPEN. Naheem opened the door to the safe and took out his P-89 Ruger and sat it on the bathrooms tiled floor.

Naheem made a few adjustments to the stacks of money that was already in the safe making room for its next thirty three thousand dollar deposit. After he placed the money in the safe with the rest, Naheem closed the door to the safe. When the door was closed the red lights danced again as they formed the word LOCKED, then the lights died.

After checking the clip of the Ruger Naheem stood and

placed the weapon in his waistband. He returned to the living room and continued the conversation where he left off.

“That nigga Kayo tryna get some purp and some cigarettes. Him and Vailz cell buddies now, I gotta get shorty another phone the last one got knocked.” Naheem explained as he stood in the middle of the living room.

Without taking his eye off the flat screen TV, Nasir uttered, “Them niggaz supposed to be on their way home don't they?”

“Yeah, Kayo go to court in two days. I ain't get a chance to holla at Vialz cause he said it was count time.”

“They gonna call back to check on that move,” Nasir knowingly stated.

Naheem readjusted his pistol.

“Let's bounce shorty, it's time to make the donuts.”

Without a response Nasir rose up off the leather lounge chair simultaneously pulling his chrome 9mm Berretta from under its cushion. He stuffed the weapon into his waistband and adjusted his green Polo shirt.

“Awight, let's shake.”

CHAPTER 3

In no time the two were out the apartment, down the stairs and out the building. They walked to Nasir's Range Rover in silence. Once inside the truck both men routinely took out and placed their weapons on their laps. Nasir brought the truck to life while pushing a few buttons on the radio until he found CD 4. Playa's Circle song Lil' Duffle Bag Boy filled the trucks interior as Nasir backed out the parking space and headed out the parking lot.

The midday traffic was light as they rode down the Alameda. Nasir was just about to try to make the yellow light at Harford Rd. when the light quickly turned red. As they sat waiting for the light to change the thunderous sounds of several dirt bikes could be heard.

"Look... The flock right there." Nasir said pointing to the source of the noise. Thirty or so dirt bikes of various sizes and colors could be seen approaching the intersection. Naheem saw an all too familiar face leading the pack.

"Hit the horn yo, there go Hook."

Hook was Naheem's cousin. He was from the westside

of Baltimore called Reisterstown. Hook was older than Naheem by a few months. He had features of what most would call a pretty boy. With his light skin complexion, curly hair and green eyes it was hard to tell he was a savaged beast.

Nasir hit the horn a few times to get Hook's attention. Hook was rolling through the intersection when he heard the horn. When he looked and saw Nasir's truck he waved his hand to the herd to continue down Harford Road as he veered to the right where Nasir's truck was. Hook pulled up to the passenger side of the truck on his blue and white Yamaha 125 facing traffic.

"Damn, I was about to ride pass you niggaz." Hook said kicking his bike into neutral.

"What's good?" Naheem asked out of the passenger window.

"Man... I had to get up with you sooner or later cause I got a move for us plus my man up the Heights tryna holla at you."

"That's what it do, just hit me." Hooks eyes roamed the truck.

"Damn Nasir, this truck like that... I might have to get me one." Hook saw the weapons on their laps.

"I see you niggaz still tote in them little ass water guns."

"This that hard body shit," Nasir spat.

Hook laughed and adjusted the bulge on the side of his hip, "I tote four fives like change for a twenty!"

The light turned green as the men shared a quick laugh. Cars behind Nasir had begun blowing their horns. Naheem told Hook, "Let me see what that bike do."

Hook backed the big bike into the crosswalk then kicked it into first gear.

The bike roared with extreme power as the front wheel jumped up in the air. Naheem and Nasir watched Hook as they rode through the light. All they could see was Hook riding on the back wheel holding the dirt bike up with his right hand and waving to the oncoming traffic with his left hand. On St. Lo Drive, Naheem said to Nasir, "That nigga nice with that bike."

"I think the nigga ride that shit in the rain." Nasir said in a joking manner as he made a left on to Sinclair Lane.

They rode the rest of the way in silence. Nasir spoke on his phone to some woman he promised to see later that night while Naheem listened to Lil' Waynes, Damn I miss my dawgs, pump out the trucks JVC speakers.

Nasir just made the turn onto Bowleys Lane when Naheem felt his phone vibrating on his hip. The screen of the phone indicated that he had a text message. After pushing a few buttons on the phone he retrieved a message from Netta that read, "Havin fun miss u ttyl."

Naheem texted back, "C U soon sexxxy."

He looked up from his phone just as Nasir made the left into Lorelly which was the name of the apartment buildings on each side of a dead end street. Nasir parked in front of the first building on the right. They both exited the vehicle and walked in the direction of the building. They entered the building and climbed one flight of stairs then stood in front of a door that read 2B. Naheem fumbled with the keys on his key ring until he found the one he was in search of.

Once in the apartment they went straight to work. This

apartment was much different from the safe house. It was completely empty with one table in the living room and two chairs. On the counter in the kitchen sat a bottle of Windex, a half full gallon jug of bleach and what looked like a dish rag. On the opposite counter close to the stove sat a small hand held processer. Nasir pulled a ten gallon storage bin to the side of the table that had been sitting in the corner.

Naheem was in the kitchen cabinets pulling out Ziploc bags, a Sifter, a digital scale with a bowl on top and a measuring cup. With the materials in hand, Naheem walked to the table and sat them down before returning to the kitchen to retrieve the hand held food processor. On the way out the kitchen with the processer in hand, Naheem stopped at the refrigerator and took out a brown paper bag then joined Nasir at the table.

"What we gonna do?" Nasir questioned as Naheem returned.

"Let's do a five. Put 2500 grams on the table." Naheem said plugging the food processer into the wall.

Nasir opened the storage bin and with the measuring cup Naheem laid on the table he began to scoop the three-in-one mixture of Benita and Quinine out of it and into the digital scales bowl. Once the scale read 2500 Nasir dumped the mixture on the table and spread it out using two playing cards that sat on the table.

Meanwhile Naheem opened the brown bag and removed two pieces of tannish gray raw heroin before dropping them in the scales bowl. The numbers on the scale raced and stopped at 510 grams.

Naheem took the smaller of the two rocks and put it in

the processor. When the top was on he held it down with one hand while pressing the little red button on the side causing the motor to turn shredding, dicing and chopping its contents. Naheem would press the button then shake the processor and push the button again. When he was done he'd lift the lid off the processor and make sure all the rocks were gone before pouring the tannish grey dust on top of the Benita and Quinine. Naheem took the same course of action with the larger rock transforming it to powder and pouring it on the mixture also. Nasir then begun mixing the ingredients together using the same two playing cards.

He stuffled the mixture back and forth trying to spread the heroin through the cut evenly. After doing that so many times Nasir stopped to allow Naheem to dump some of the cut heroin into the measuring cup using one of the playing cards, then he dumped the cut heroin from the measuring cup into the sifter.

Naheem allowed the cut heroin to escape the bottom, freely falling into a pile as he gently tapped the rim of the metal sifter. After doing that with all the cut heroin twice it was time to bag it up.

Little fish scale like crystals could be seen in the three kilos' in front of the men. Excellent with arithmetic, Naheem knew that twenty-five grams of the scrambled heroin had a street value of one thousand dollars so he asked Nasir, “what you tryna do for Tye?”

Naheem didn't say a word, he just began scooping the scrambled heroin into the scales bowl. With every pile he dumped into the bowl the numbers on the scale rose, he only slowed when the numbers read 986. From there he sprinkled the rest of the scrambled heroin slowly not trying to exceed the thousand gram mark. After a few baby scoops the scales screen finally read one thousand. Nasir detached the bowl from the scale and poured the substance into a Ziploc bag then sat the kilo of scrambled heroin to the side while Naheem attached the bowl back to the scale. Continuing the same process, Naheem weighed out fifteen hundred grams that would be for Nephew.

"The remaining five-hundred ten grams is for Dutch," Naheem explained.

Nasir pulled a black permanent marker from his pocket and waited for Naheem to speak.

"Put 40 on Tye bag, 60 on Neph's and 20 on Dutch's. I did it like that cause this is the last of it. This should hold everybody for at least two days. That'll give me enough time to get up with Roberto."

Nasir wrote on the bags of heroin as Naheem began the cleanup process. They cleaned everything with bleach and put all the utensils back where they got them from and left the apartment with three bags of heroin.

In the truck Naheem placed the grocery bag containing the heroin on the floor by his feet while Nasir headed to the next destination.

* * * * * * *

The two were indulged in a little small talk as they rode down McElderly Street. Nasir made the right onto Streeper riding past two touters on one side of the street scratching and in half nods shouting, "Red Monkey! Getcha Red

Monkey right here ya'll!"

On the other corner was a young man with a walkie talkie that served as a lookout. Another young guy wearing a white tank top with a black bandanna on his head could be seen on the roof of the row houses pacing back and forth while talking into his walkie talkie. The inside of the block was pure pandemonium. People covered the small block in search of the drug that tore households apart and snatched the morals and principals from the souls of men. This very narcotic that the people were in search of devoured its prey from the inside out claiming victory over anyone who dared to challenge its massive grip. Women would fall from grace and be stripped of their pride. Mentally defeated by their heavy weight powder contender, women would often times leave their children for the streets to raise while in search for the love of their life, HEROIN.

The history of the inescapable physical, psychological and eternal death that was being sold in those capsules proved its' uncaring assault on its victims was a fight rarely lost and as a result, the poisonous capsules were in high demand.

Nasir drove through the crowded block and stopped at the intersection of Streeper and Jefferson. On the corner to the left was two more touters yelling, "We got that Monkey ya'll, RED MONKEY OUT!!!"

To the left a young man stood with a walkie talkie in hand, the young man was shielded from the sun by a blue awning with white letters that read Nelly's Deli. Just as Nasir made the right onto Jefferson Nephew appeared out of the store turning a bottled water up to his mouth. Nasir got to the next corner and made a left on Kenwood then parked. Naheem took the bag of heroin that had the number 60 written on it and placed it underneath his chair while placing the rest of the heroin under the driver seat. They exited the vehicle and started towards the corner where they just saw Nephew.

At the store Naheem and Nasir exchanged dap with Nephew before Nasir spoke.

“What's the holdup Lil' Daddy, why the block so congested?”

“I thought it might've been better if I let the crowd build up so Stoney ain't have to keep running back and forth to get packs. I got three hundred pills left, I'm only hittin once,” Nephew said with confidence in his decision.

“That's awight but don't make it a habit, hit’em and get’em gone,” Nasir explained.

Naheem cut in, “Dig this Neph.... I got a brick and a half, can you handle that?”

Eyes wide as dinner plates Nephew countered, “One and a half? That's what the fuck I'm talkin about! A nigga getting promotions out this bitch. What's my number?”

“42... you keep 18.”

“You already know my nig,” Nephew said rubbing his hands together. Nasir handed Nephew the keys to his truck with instructions.

“Look under the passenger seat, you gon see a bag that say 60, that's you. Don't forget to lock the truck.”

With no more words exchanged, Nephew took the key's and walked toward Kenwood while talking into his walkie talkie. A few seconds later Stoney ran out the alley screaming, "Everybody in the alley, Red Monkey hittin in five minutes. Cop and Bop, money in hand, no singles, no jingles!"

At the same time Nasir and Naheem noticed that the corner men on each end of the block begun to walk towards each other herding the crowd into alleys on both sides of the street.

A light skinned woman with jet black hair wearing a black form fitting Roberto Cavalli dress that stopped well above her knees came out of a house on Jefferson. She seductively sashayed in the direction of Naheem and Nasir. She spoke only when she reached the same side of the street.

"What's up Naheem, what's up Nasir?"

"What's up Lisa." Both men managed to say admiring the sight of Lisa's curvaceous figure.

"Damn Naheem, I hope you taste as good as you look."

"I just bet you do," Naheem uttered evading Lisa's advances. Pressing on she asked, "You tryna hook up later?"

Without the slightest bit of thought, Naheem responded, "Naw... I'm busy."

"Awight then, when?" Lisa quizzed with a hand on her hip as if she demanded an answer.

"When I get time."

"Yeah awight, whatever then." Lisa said obviously upset about being brushed off.

"I'll holla at you later Nasir." She huffed.

"Do that." Nasir retorted as Lisa casually strolled back in the direction from which she came putting an extra sway in her hips.

Naheem diverted his eyes from Lisa's voluptuous backside.

“She think she got all the damn sense. She ain't wanna give a nigga no ass when I was out here on balls and knuckles now she got some wrap.”

“I'll take her off your hands for you.”

“Do you.” Naheem said without a care.

Just as the two ended their conversation a pearl white Cadillac CTS came down Streeper and stopped at the corner in front of them. The mirror tinted window of the Cadillac came down on its passenger side revealing Nephew on the driver side.

“Yo, I'm about to go cap this shit up so I can get it out today.” Nephew said as he tossed Nasir his keys.

“Awight shorty, handle your business.” Naheem said of Nephew’s departure.

The window went up and Nephew made a left on Jefferson and rode until he was out of sight.

“Let's bounce before Stoney Lil' ass hit the crowd.” Nasir said as he turned and started walking in the direction his truck was in with Naheem a few steps behind.

When they got into the truck, Naheem grabbed the heroin he placed under the driver's chair and put it back on the floor by his feet before Nasir pulled off.

* * * * * * *

They passed a McDonalds that was to the right as they rode down Broadway towards Hartford Road. Nasir made a left turn into a Wendy's parking lot that sat on the corners of Broadway and Harford. Nasir parked and shut the truck off then dialed some numbers on his phone. A few seconds later he spoke into the phone.

"Yeah.., what's up? Meet me at the girl Wendy house."

Nasir disconnected the call. A few moments later Tye could be seen standing on the corner of Harford road waiting for the light to change so he could cross the street. The light finally turned red and the traffic ceased allowing him to cross. Tye walked into the Wendy's parking lot and saw Nasir's truck off to the right. He approached the trucks rear passenger door and hopped in.

"What it is?"

Nasir responded first, "You been holdin your spot down so we gon take you off salary and go 70/30 with you. It's your job to pay the shop. You'll touch your paper every day, play fair with your people."

Tye's brown eyes bucked, and he licked his full lips, "Man, when this go into effect!"

"Right now." Naheem passed the bag of heroin to the back seat. "That should hold you for two days, give me 28 and keep 12. Can you handle that?" Naheem asked looking over the parking lot.

With his future looking much brighter Tye joyously announced, "Hell yeah I can handle it just watch me work."

Tye put the bag of heroin in his waistband in front of his pants. Naheem opened the door and Nasir followed suit with Tye in step behind them. They crossed Harford and walked down Bonaparte to the first block which was Aiken street.

As they made the left onto the 2100 block of Aiken a line of addicts waited to be served by a young man who looked to be in his late teens or early twenties. Tye ran up the steps and into a house. Nasir and Naheem just looked around and waited for Tye to come back out. Naheem was just about to sit down on the steps when he saw a book on the steps where he intended to sit. Naheem held the book in the air.

"Who fuckin book is this?"

Nobody answered so he spoke again louder than the last time.

"I said, who- fuckin- book- is- this?"

Hearing the commotion outside Tye came to the porch the same time the young man serving the addicts responded, "That's my book... why what's up?"

Nasir and Tye looked at Naheem with raised eyebrows. Naheem told Tye, "Shut it down for a minute."

Confused, he informed the line of forty or so people, "We on hold for ten minutes."

Some of the people got in their cars and waited while others paced the small block or just stood in place.

Naheem pointed to the young man, "Aye Tye... who's that nigga?"

"That's my cousin Angie's boyfriend, his name Tavon. He use to work up at the McDonald's, I gave him a job on the strength of my people's."

Naheem called out to the man across the street, "Aye Tavon... let me holla at you rea1 quick."

Unaware of why Naheem was calling, Tavon crossed the street to where Naheem was.

"You say this your book?"

"Yeah why... what..."

Before Tavon could complete his sentence, Naheem threw a right jab that landed on his chin. Tavon was caught off guard and fell to one knee quickly bouncing back to his feet as if to charge Naheem. When Tavon looked up he was staring down the barrel of Nasir's Berretta and he stopped in his tracks. The look in Nasir's eyes spoke volumes. Tye stood astounded as the whole scene unfolded. Naheem clinched his teeth.

"Get your bitch ass off this block and don't let me see you around here no more."

Tavon saw he was in a no win situation. He peered at Naheem for a second then turned and walked away feeling the side effects of Naheems' strike. When Tavon was out of sight Nasir placed the Berretta back in his waistband.

"What the fuck was that about?"

Naheem held the book up with his left hand. "We in the streets… we got codes. This nigga got a book the rat bitch Vicky Stinger wrote. That tell me he support rats!"

Still disturbed by the brief conflict, Naheem looked at Tye.

"That nigga fired, hire somebody else."

Tye nodded his head. Naheem and Nasir turned and strolled back to the truck.

Once inside the truck Nasir insisted, "We gon have to dump shorty."

"I doubt it." Naheem asserted.

"Man you knocked the shit out his lil ass."

"We'll play it by ear." Naheem murmured.

“Awight.” Nasir headed towards South Baltimore.

* * * * * * *

30 minutes later they were on Patapsco. Naheems phone vibrated, although he wasn't familiar with the number he answered anyway. A womens voice said, “Hi... can I speak to Naheem?”

“Yeah this me.”

“Oh... Okay, this is Sherry. I'm calling for Kayo.”

“Awight, when can you meet me?”

“Anytime is good for me.”

“What side of town you on?”

“I live in Woodlawn.”

“That's perfect. Can you meet me at the Winsor Inn at 9:30 tonight.”

“Yeah, that's good for me. I'll meet you there.”

“Awight, I'll see you then.”

“Okay.” Sherry said before the line died.

Nasir pulled into a gas station on 9th and Patapsco. Both men exited the vehicle and walked inside the gas station. The gas station was empty so Nasir went straight to the counter.

“Get me twenty on five.”

Nasir handed the Arab looking man with the sleek black hair a twenty dollar bill. After the Arab guy pressed a few buttons on the cash register Naheem stepped up and pointed to the cartons of cigarettes behind the counter.

“Let me get a carton of Newport one hundreds.”

The Arab spun and grabbed the carton then he began to

ring it up when Naheem continued, “You ain't got no prepaid phones?”

“We only have these,” The Arab gestured to a rack of AT&T go phones.

“Give me one and fifty dollars in minutes.”

“One ten forty five is the total sir.”

The Arab’s english was nearly perfect. Naheem paid for the contents and they walked out the gas station. Nasir leaned on the truck pumping the gas while Naheem climbed in the truck. Naheem told Nasir, “Yo… Call Dutch. Tell ‘em meet us over here.”

With the gas pump in one hand Nasir grabbed his phone with his free hand and commenced to dialing. In the truck Naheem put his Ruger under the chair and relaxed. After pumping the gas Nasir walked around the truck and got in when he saw Dutch coming out of 9th Street crossing Patapsco into the gas stations lot. Dutch jumped in the back seat.

“What it is?”

“You already know soljah, slow groovin like a real pimp.” Naheem said.

“You the man, I'd cut both my hands off for one of yours.” Nasir jokingly told Dutch.

“It's still hot out here'?” Naheem asked using extreme caution.

“I mean, the jump outs comin through every so often but we good, just gotta keep our eyes open.”

Naheem broke down the numbers as he handed the heroin to Dutch.

“Look homez, this 20 should last you two days. You

owe 14... It's 10 grams over for you to tee-off with. I figure you gon need to drop some testers to get your crowd back.

"That's just what I needed, I'm about to put the word out now."

As Dutch got out the truck Naheem stopped him.

"Who got the Haze out here?"

"What you looking for?"

"Just an ounce." Naheem's tone was matter of factly.

"My man E.J. got some kill, you want me to hit him?"

"Yeah, holla at him for me."

Naheem opened the trucks door. Nasir started to get out also. Naheem reminded him, "Yo, leave the hammer in the ride. It's shaky out here."

"Damn, I'm trippin!" Nasir said.

He slipped his gun under his seat and the three men walked across Patapsco to 9th and Dutch ran in a house to put the heroin up. Shortly after, he joined Naheem and Nasir out front.

"E.J. on the way around here, he say he local."

Moments later a white S-type Acura pulled two cars up from where the three gentlemen stood.

"That's yo right there." Dutch said as the man stepped out the car.

Dutch introduced Naheem and E.J. then they walked to E.J.'s car to talk while Dutch and Nasir stood two cars away. From where Nasir stood he could see an exchange between the two.

E.J. leaned on his car with his back toward the street while Naheem faced the street. An black Dodge Charger slowly rolled down the street then stopped directly on the other side of E.J.'s car. The limo tinted passenger side window came down and the occupant spoke to no one in particular.

"You know where Patapsco at?"

As E.J. leaned up off the car to answer, the back window of the passenger side came down and shots rang out.

Boom Boom... Boom Boom Boom.

Naheem dropped to the side of the Acura. The first shot hit E.J. high in the left shoulder causing him to spin from the bullets impact and fall. Sounds of a second pistol could be heard along with the deep hollow Booms. Dutch and Nasir hit the ground in just enough time to see a bullet slam into the car window shattering it and sending little pieces of glass everywhere. The Chargers tires screeched as the car regained its traction, speeding to the end of 9th making a wide right turn onto Patapsco.

E.J. laid on the ground and held his left shoulder as he emitted a loud ear splitting cry.

"Oh shit.. I'm hit... Oh shit!"

Naheem got up from the cover of E.J.'s car briskly walking two cars down to Nasir and Dutch who were wiping themselves of shattered glass.

"Get dude to a hospital. Don't let the ambulance pick him up here cause that'll only make it hotter around here." Naheem advised.

Dutch walked over to E.J. who was now standing.

"Give me your keys."

E.J. complied as Dutch walked around the car to get in the driver side. E.J. quickly got in the passenger side. As they made the left onto Patapsco, Naheem and Nasir could be seen hopping in the truck.

"What the fuck was all that about?" Nasir asked as he slowly pulled out the gas stations parking lot trying not to bring any unwanted attention to them.

"I don't know. We gon have to get back up with Dutch on that." Naheem said.

"Where we at?" Came Nasir's query.

Naheem thought for a minute, "Go back around Streeper."

Grabbing for his phone Naheem noticed one of them was missing.

"Shit... I dropped my bitch box... Fuck it."

Naheem grabbed his remaining phone and scrolled through it until he found the name X. He sent X a short text message that consisted of a single question mark then placed the phone back on his hip.

"I just texted Roberto. Hopefully he get right back."

"Last time it took him four days to holla back." Nasir said.

"He ain't never get back at me the same day."

Naheem felt his phone vibrating. Caught off guard for a moment thinking that the call was possibly Roberto, he instantly thought better of it reminding himself that Roberto never spoke on phones. Without looking at the caller ID he answered.

"What's up?"

Naheem recognized the voice on the other end as Hook.

"Aye... I'm kinda busy right now but some shit just came up with that move I holla'd at you about. Ima be done what I'm doin' around nine. I need to get with you today."

Hearing the seriousness in Hooks voice Naheem said, “Awight, meet me at the Winsor Inn at nine-nine thirty, that's good for you?”

“That's cool, I'll see you then.”

CHAPTER 4

On Streeper, Naheem and Nasir sat on some steps and watched the heavy traffic flow in and out of the block. Nasir was busy talking to a young woman named Kia who seemed to hold his attention. Nephew paced the block from corner to corner occasionally barking orders into his walkie talkie. A crowd of forty or more people developed due to the shop being on hold awaiting the next pack. In the crowd Naheem thought he spotted a familiar face. He peered at the older lady in the mist of the crowd. Hoping he really wasn't seeing what he thought, Naheem stopped Nephew who was about to walk by and ordered. He pointed in the direction of the woman.

"Bring her over here."

Nephew spoke into his walkie talkie, "Yo, corner one, get auntie out the crowd that's wearin the brown sweatshirt."

Seconds later one of the young men that stood on the corner of Streeper and Jefferson left his post to retrieve the woman from the growing crowd.

The young man said something to the lady as he began

to walk her over to where Nephew stood. At 85 degrees the woman wore a brown sweatshirt that was clearly too big with a faded pair of jeans that looked as if they never seen a single wash. Her hair was unkept and matted together from lack of attention. When she looked up and saw Naheem she looked as if she'd seen a ghost. She then began to try to straighten her poorly kept clothes brushing at lint that was never there and rubbing her hands through her kinky hair.

The woman’s attempt to beautify herself enraged Naheem but he held his composure. Her eyes were glossy and yellow. Now standing in front of Nephew, the woman stood as her escort walked back to his post. Naheem jumped up off the steps and snatched the woman by her arm marching her up the street away from everybody before letting her arm loose. Naheem glared into his son's mother's frightened eyes.

“Michelle what the fuck is wrong with you?”

At 23 years of age Michelle looked 50.

“What you mean?” She grumbled averting Naheem’s eye contact.

“What I mean? What the fuck you think I mean? Ain’t nobody seen you in two years and when you do pop up you in a dope line, that's what the fuck I mean.” Naheem said now unable to control his anger.

Michelle’s mouse grey complexion made Naheem think that she might be infected with H.I.V or A.I.D.S.

“I'm doin me Naheem, that's all I'm doin, I'm livin my life.”

Naheem grabbed her left wrist and raised the sleeve of her filthy sweatshirt surveying the inside of her forearm, track marks were left from where she had been intravenously sending heroin into her veins.

"Damn, you spike'in, too?"

Before she could answer Naheem asked, "What about Prince?"

"He good, you got him. You gon make sure he straight." Michelle murmured as she pulled the sleeve down over her malnourished track riddled arm.

Naheem's heart felt as if it weighed a thousand pounds. Now he knew Michelle had gone off the deep end. The chances of her recovery was slim to none.

The movement of the corner men herding the people in the alley indicated that the pack had arrived. Mentally pulling himself back together Naheem pulled out a wad of cash peeling off a hundred dollar bill and handed it to Michelle.

"Live your life yo."

When he placed the bill in her hand she looked at it and made an effort to hug him causing Naheem to take a step back, silently looking into her glassy eyes.

"Thanks." She said before trotting back down the block to where the drugs were being distributed.

Naheem walked back to the steps in deep thought. Nephew was back running the block and the girl Nasir had been entertaining was gone. Nasir didn't bother to ask about Naheem's heated conversation with Michelle. He overheard bits and pieces of their exchange but he figured when and if Naheem felt like talking about it he would.

Michelle purchased her heroin and came out the alley and met up with a much older woman.

"Girl, what you was talkin to the boss man about?"

Quickly walking away with her five capsules of heroin in hand Michelle told the woman, "That's my baby father."

Disbelieving what she'd just been told the older lady said, "Uhuh... tell me anything girl. He can be my baby daddy too then."

They bent the corner and was out of sight.

"This shit is crazy." Naheem mumbled to himself as he shook his head.

"Let's run up Greenmount real quick and holla at Dinkles." Nasir said as he stood up off the steps stretching his legs. Naheem didn't answer.

"Yo... Let's hit the Mount." Nasir reiterated.

Snapping out of a day dream Naheem stood and stretched his legs also before they made their way to the truck.

* * * * * * *

Dinkles had been friends with Naheem since the fifth grade when they both attended Harford Heights Elementary. Dinkles aunt raised him but when she got strung out on crack he sought guidance in the streets. Ultimately he dropped out of school his 8th grade year to sell drugs full time. Even though Naheem was still in school the two remained close through the years to come.

One day at a car wash on North and Milton, Naheem and Nasir saw Dinkles. Naheem introduced the two, Nasir took a liking to Dinkles because they had alot in common. Nasir and Dinkles started selling crack in the 2600 block of

Boone. Nasir bought the coke and Dinkles rocked it up and put it out on the streets. Naheem liked the relationship that Nasir and Dinkles formed.

Nasir parked on Boone street and he and Naheem got out. Boone was two blocks long, with both blocks being dead ends. Dinkles had his young soldiers on alert at all times on the corners between the two dead end blocks. In Boone street a small dice game was in session.

"Can I get a fade." Dinkles could be heard saying as he shook a pair of red dice.

"Shoot nigga." A young man named Tay-Tay said throwing a twenty on the ground and stepping on it.

"I like his come out for fifty." The man known as Manny-El announced trying to secure a bet.

Tay-Tay was a ruthless killer, at sixteen years of age he had a graveyard under his belt. He was loyal to Dinkles and only Dinkles although Manny-El was his older cousin. As far as Tay-Tay was concerned he was Manny-El's older cousin. He was wilder than Manny-El making him appear to be soft.

Manny-Els was more of a peoples person, he got along with everybody. He was 21 years of age, he and Dinkles grew up together. Although he wasn't as aggressive as his younger cousin he still held his own in the streets. Unlike most of Manny-El friends, his decision to enter the street life was his own. He graduated from Dunbar High School. Manny-El mother was a retired school teacher. His father died when he was thirteen of asbestosis from working at Bethlehem Steel's Metal Plant. After high school, Manny-El lost sight of his goal which was to go to Penn State for a

BA in accounting. The streets magnetic pull lured Manny-El with its fast cars, fast women and fast money.

As Naheem and Nasir walked up on the men Tay-Tay was the first to see them.

"What's up Big Nigga?" He asserted causing Dinkles and Manny-El to turn.

"Ain't shit Lil Daddy." Nasir responded.

Naheem walked up to Dinkles giving him some dap. Nasir continued, "What you niggaz up to?"

"Huggin the block." Tay-Tay said.

Dinkles declared, "I'm out her fuckin these niggaz life up."

Nasir held his phone to his ear as he walked away from the others to take a call. Naheem was discussing the possibility of giving Dinkles heroin when Nasir came back to where the men stood. He leaned over and whispered in Naheem's ear, "Dutch say he got some word about that demonstration."

"Oh yeah!"

"Yeah, I told him we would meet him tomorrow at Moe's on Richie Highway. Oh... He said his man good too."

"That's what it is."

Naheem thought of revenge. Manny-El interrupted the side bar, "You heard from Kayo lately?"

"I talked to him earlier. He say he go to court Monday."

"That's all he said?" Manny-El quizzed.

"Yup, that and he want me to meet a broad later."

As time went on Tay-Tay left to go to his post which was listening to a police scanner in a vacant house across the street. A little while later Manny- Els girlfriend Jaleesa came to pick him up. Naheem looked at the time on his phone and realized that a little more than an hour had passed. He looked at Nasir and said, “Take me to my car yo.”

After they exchanged daps with Dinkles, Naheem and Nasir got back in the truck and headed to the safe house.

In the safe-house parking lot Nasir drove all the way to the end and parked next to Naheem’s car. Naheem got out Nasir's truck grabbing the carton of cigarettes and the phone from the back seat and the ounce of Haze out the glove compartment. He put the Haze in the same bag as the carton and the phone then put the bag in his car on the passenger side floor. Naheem walked to the truck after pushing the trunk release button on his key ring. The huge trunk was empty bearing nothing but a black Nike backpack. Naheem got the backpack and shut the trunk and walked over to Nasir who was standing in front of the apartment building holding it's door open.

In the apartment Nasir sat on the loveseat and cut the entertainment system on. Naheem walked to the bathroom with the backpack in hand. Once there, he opened the safe taking out all the money that it held and placed it in the backpack stack by stack. When the safe was empty Naheem placed his Ruger in and closed it. Back in the living room Naheem asked, “What's on your agenda?'

“After I finish makin my rounds, Ima hit the strip club for a minute. I told the lil chick Champagne I'd come see her dance tonight.”

“Where she strip at?” Naheem asked not really

interested.

"She use to be in Foxy Ladies now she in Norma Jean's. You rollin early, what you got planned?"

"I gotta meet Hook and see what type shit he talkin then I got to see the girl for Kayo. Ima just go home and chill after that."

"Awight then my nig, I'll holla in the A.M."

"That's what it is." Naheem said with the cash filled backpack in hand making his way toward the door.

When he got to his car he opened the door and threw the backpack on the passenger seat and started the car. The car clock read 8:36. Naheem knew he'd be a little late for the meeting with Hook.

"Fuck it, Ima take the back road." He thought while pulling out of the parking lot.

* * * * * * *

Naheem sat at a red light on Winsor Mill and Forrest Park waiting for the light to change when he saw a black Charger pull into the gas station across the street. Just seeing the same kind of car that shot at him earlier infuriated him. Naheem watched to see if he recognized any of the occupants of the vehicle. The light turned green and Naheem slowly rolled through the intersection eyeing the Charger when a young woman got out the driver side and walked into the gas station. Another woman got out the passenger side and placed the gas nozzle inside of the cars tank. Seeing two women Naheem resumed speed up Winsor Mill for another mile.

When he was approaching the Winsor Inn Naheem saw that the parking lot was packed with all sorts of cars. He rode through the parking lot in search of a good spot to the right. Naheem backed into the parking spot and grabbed the plastic bag off the passenger side floor and the backpack of cash off the passenger seat as he got out. It was still nice outside at 9:15 at night, Naheem could smell the strong stench of Haze that hung in the air as he walked to the back of the car to put the backpack in the trunk. When Naheem got to the front door he was met by a 6 foot 4 inch 375 pound man wearing a black shirt that read SECURITY in white letters. When Naheem approached the bouncer he handed him a fifty dollar bill and proceeded on past him with the plastic bag in hand.

Inside the Winsor Inn loud rebel cries of Buju Banton could be heard blasting out the speakers. Naheem saw Hook sitting at the end of the bar talking to an attractive bartender name Tweety. Tweety spoke first as Naheem sat next to Hook placing the bag on the bar.

"Hey Naheem, how you been?"

"I'm good," Naheem replied with a half smile.

"Can I get you something?"

"Yeah, get me a Goose and pineapple."

Tweety turned to fill the order as Hook vented, "Man, she still ain't tryna give me no ass. She keep talkin that relationship shit."

"Who Tweety?"

"Yeah."

Hook was about to continue but Tweety appeared and sat Naheem's drink in front of him. Naheem gave her a twenty and told her to keep the change. Hook grinned at Naheem. “I got a tip for you too. Stop playin with me girl.”

“Boy please.” Tweety said with a smile then turned and continued to tend to the bar.

Hook began to speak as Naheem took a sip of his drink.

“I got a move for us. I'm almost sure that between money and coke we can come off with a mill easy.”

Hearing the possibility of a free million dollars caught Naheem’s attention. Now he was listening attentively as Hook continued. “I was fuckin a Lil chick name Reeva a few months ago and she hooked me up with her brother. I started getting coke from him but he was stuntin like he ain't have it like that, I guess he was feelin me out. Make a long story short he tryna give me ten bricks. All he want is $19,750 a joint.”

“Where the mill come in at?” Naheem questioned trying to gain a better understanding.

“Reeva use to say lil shit about the nigga, like how he got his money up and she don't know why he still in the game and how the nigga got a spot down in Atlanta. If worst come to worst we still got five keys a piece. The nigga holdin on the low. I know he got at least a mill in the cut somewhere.”

The phone on Naheem's hip began to vibrate.

“Hold up for a minute.”

He put the phone to his ear. A female's voice on the other end said, “Hello.”

“Yeah.”

“I'm outside.” It was Sherry.

“Awight, come in. I'm sitting at the bar.”

“Okay.”

From the Winsor Inn parking lot Sherry walked straight to the bar and instantly recognized Naheem. She spoke as she took a seat on the other side of him.

“I do remember you, I couldn't picture your face at first.”

“You want a drink?” Naheem asked as he slid the bag to her. Sherry took the bag and looked inside to examine its contents.

“No I'm good, I have to work in the morning but thanks anyway.” Naheem handed her a thousand dollars and she smiled.

“Thank you."

“That shit ain't nothin. Call me when my niggaz need somethin.” Naheem said and took another sip of his drink.

Sherry stepped down off the bar stool and grabbed the bag Naheem had just given her as she made her way out the lounge. Naheem looked over at Hook to continue their conversation when he noticed Hook in a daze staring over the bar. He followed Hook's eyes and saw that Tweety was leaning over the bar across from them letting the enchanting sounds of Bounty Killa take over her body. Her back was seductively arched as she leaned on the bar, she swayed her behind causing it to bounce. Naheem snapped Hook out of his trance.

“Damn nigga, you droolin on the bar!”

“I need some of that.”

Naheem frowned then went back to their previous conversation.

“How is this shit goin down?”

"He always meet me at the gas station on McClean and Northern Parkway around 12 or 1 O'clock. He got a lil townhouse over in Dutch Village where he keep the coke. I just don't know how much in there. All we gotta do is get him from the gas station across the street to Dutch Village. Once we got him in the house we can work."

Naheem thought for a second before speaking, "When you tryna move?"

"Tonight."

"Damn that's short notice."

"I know, that's why I told you I had to see you tonight."

Naheem sighed, "Awight, I'm in."

"I need you to be at the gas station on McClean at 12:30. All you have to do is follow my lead."

"Awight... 12:30, I got it." Naheem got off the tall stool. "Ima go home first and put this shit up and I'll meet you there."

Moments later when Naheem got to his car his phone vibrated. When he checked it he saw he had a text message from Nasir that read, "Holla in the A.M. ASAP."

Nasir never texted Naheem like that so he called him right back.

"What's up? I thought you was in for the night." Nasir said over loud music.

"What that text about?"

"Tye just hit my phone and said the lil nigga you bust off on runnin around talkin about he got five stacks for a nigga to holla at you."

Naheem laughed. "Get the fuck outta here! That lil broke bitch. Five stacks? I'm worth more than that."

“Tye say he don't want nothin to come Angie way that's why he putting us on point.”

“Awight, I’ll handle it.”

“That's what it do.” Nasir said and disconnected the line.

Wanting to leave the grind of the streets out of his home life, Naheem softened his mood as he drove listening to Sade.

Nasir’s message about Tavon made Naheem more cautious than normal. During the drive home Naheem made sure he was not being followed. A little while later Naheem pulled into his condo’s garage next to Netta’s BMW. He cut the car off and hit the trunk release on his keyring. Naheem grabbed the backpack and walked into the building. Once in the condo Naheem looked at the time on his phone. It was 10:05.

The familiar scent of Netta’s Givenchy fragrance filled his nostrills as Naheem approached the bedroom. The crooning voices of Dru Hill flowed out the hidden speakers. Naheem stood in the doorway leading into his bedroom. He allowed his eyes to adjust to the dim lighting. A smile spread across Naheem's face as he took in the scene. Wearing burgandy laced boy shorts and a matching bra Netta lay in the bed waiting for Naheem. On the glass and chrome table beside the bed a magnum bottle of Rose Moet sat in a bucket of ice. Beside it was a glass bowl of chocolate covered strawberries from Mixologist Treats and two flute glass. Without saying a word Naheem dropped the backpack and walked into the outstretched arms of his woman. Netta stood, “I still hungry Da-Da.”

She gave him her tongue then reluctantly broke the

embrace and slowly began to undress him. Naheem allowed himself to be undressed while admiring his woman's perfect body. Netta filled both glasses with wine and began to feed her man strawberries. She looked down to see Naheem's full erection and whispered, "I think we need to do something about that."

Naheem nodded. Sitting on the bed, he leaned back on to his elbows. He watched as Netta emptied her glass and took him into her mouth. Naheem tensed at the cold feel of the liquid then the heat of her mouth. The combination was overwhelming as he laid flat on his back. Netta groped his scrotum in her hand gently messaging them as she attempted to take his full length in her mouth. She gagged once then maintained a slow steady up-down rhythm. Not wanting to cum yet, Naheem laid her on her back and eased her soaked boy shorts off. He sat comfortably between her legs then began to lick and suck her clitoris while inserting a finger slowly in and out of her vagina. Netta's eye's rolled back into her head.

"Oh… my… gawwd ba... baby I'm cum... miiin."

She tried desperately to wiggle from Naheem's grasp. That only spurred him on as he was intent on bringing her to a powerful climax. He felt her body jerk then go limp as her womanly juices flowed freely. As he kissed the inside of her thigh's he could still feel Netta trembling. Naheem then turned her over and began to kiss the reverse side of her knees and her back while allowing her trembles to subside and catch her breath. Naheem then pulled Netta to him as he laid on his back. She slowly straddled him taking him inside of her. Naheem felt the walls of her vagina contract around him as she slowly and steadily rode him.

“Mmmmmm,” she moaned into his mouth as they kissed and explored each other mouth with their tongues.

Turning her onto her stomach, Naheem entered Netta from behind. He started with slow strokes at first, then feeling his own seed rising he increased his tempo and pounded into her giving her every inch of himself. Netta gasped, “Ahhh yesss.”

She met Naheem stroke for stroke. Their passionate lovemaking was fueled by Naheem's anger and frustration with the streets and by his love for Netta. They came together and collapsed. Naheem pulled her into his arms and held her as they dozed off.

Naheem awoke from his somber still holding Netta in his arms. She slept soundly. Naheem crept out of bed looking for his phone that was still hooked on to his pants on the floor. It was 11:45, Naheem knew he had to hurry. He took a ten minute shower and began to dress on the side of the bed trying not to wake Netta. Naheem put his black Robin jeans on and a pair of socks then he got up to retrieve his black Nike boots and black Lacosta shirt. He returned to the bed and Netta murmured still half sleep, “Where you goin baby?”

“I gotta go pick Hook up, his car got towed. I'll be right back Cupcake.” Naheem pulled the shirt over his head and buttoned it's three buttons.

He then walked over and kissed Netta softly on her forehead. Suddenly noticing the backpack of cash still on the floor, he walked over to it, picked it up and took it to the walk in closet and placed it on the overhead shelf. Then he went to Netta's side of the closet and grabbed a Christian Louboutin shoe box.

Naheem opened the shoe box and took out a large chrome.44 Desert Eagle and stuffed it in his waistband. Soon Naheem was out the door and on his way. He hoped all went as planned.

* * * * * * *

Naheem drove down McClean and made a right into a small shopping center behind the gas station. He parked and walked around to the front of the gas station. Just as he got to the front Hook came out the gas station and walked right by him as if he didn't know him. Hook walked around to the side of the gas station into a blind spot. Naheem waited a second and thought about his next move. He looked around the completely empty gas station and thought "fuck it" as he walked in the same direction as Hook. When Naheem got to the side of the gas station's blind spot he saw Hook's smoke gray Corvette ZR-1 alongside of a Cadillac DTS with what appeared to be Hook on the passenger side and another man on the driver side.

Hook and a dealer he knew as Sean sat in Sean's DTS making future plans. Hook put a green duffle bag containing ten kilo's on the backseat. A man in a black shirt walked in front of the car. Sean tried to pull his gun out. Hook stopped him by placing a .45 in his ribcage then he removed the gun and dropped it on the passenger side floor by his feet. Naheem walked around on the driver side and opened the back door and got in behind Sean who was now whining.

“Hook man, what's all this about?”

“All I want is the money and the coke. Don't play games, just give us the shit and we out. Drive to that little townhouse you got over in Dutch Village.”

“Please don't kill me man, all I got is --,” before Sean could finish Naheem whacked him on the right side of the head with his Desert Eagle.

“Shut up and drive bitch.”

“Ahhh,” Sean started the car.

Naheem leaned forward, “We gon let you go when we get what we want.”

Sean drove across the street to the first court in Dutch Village parking six townhouses from the end. Hook still had his gun in Sean’s side. He told Sean to take the keys out the ignition and hand them to Naheem.

“Who in there?” Hook asked Sean.

“Nobody man… Ain’t nobody in there.” Sean cried.

“Awight we gon go in there and if you start acting stupid Ima knock your fucking face off. Which one of these keys fit the door?”

“It's the silver one.”

Hook turned to Naheem, “Yo, see if that key work.”

Naheem slid out the back seat and walked up to the door and put the key inside the lock. He turned it and lightly pushed the door a few inches and walked back to the car. Hook told Naheem to grab the duffle bag off the back seat and handed him Sean's gun telling him to put it in the bag also. With the duffle bag in his left hand, Naheem closed the back door. He pulled a .44 from his waistband and told Sean to get out.

At 12:45 in the morning nobody was outside, it was extremely quiet. Sean's townhouse was the only one in the court where lights were on. The surrounding darkness made it easy to see the light inside the kitchen. Sean opened his door as Hook hopped out of the passenger side with his .45 down beside his leg. Sean walked into the townhouse first followed by Hook then Naheem.

Naheem dropped the duffle bag on the floor and Hook made Sean sit in one of the four chairs that surrounded the table in the dining room to the left. Naheem searched the kitchen until he found a roll of grey duct tape. Hook held his gun to Sean's head while Naheem taped his ankles to the legs of the chair. Sean stuttered, "Ma.. ma... man pl... please don't k... ki.. kill m... me."

As Naheem taped Sean's hands behind the chair Hook answered Sean's plea. "I told you, just don't act crazy and everybody gon live to see the sun come up."

Naheem demanded, "Where the rest of the coke?"

"I got ten keys in the back of the dryer."

Hook looked at Naheem and nodded towards the kitchen. Naheem turned and walked inside it. Pulling the dryer from the wall, he saw a square opening at the bottom of the machine. Naheem pulled the dryer all the way out and searched the back of it. He pulled out one kilo at a time then pushed the dryer back up against the wall. He brought the ten kilo's to the dining room and dropped them on the floor.

"I wouldn't play games Hook, can I go now?" Sean

begged.

Naheem glared at him, “Hold up yo, where the rest of the shit at?”

“That's all of it I swear on my kids.”

“Kill that nigga Hook, he playin games.”

“No, no, no please man look, I got a little bit more coke upstairs in a tool box in the hallway closet.”

Naheem ran up the stairs and came back with a metal toolbox and sat it on the floor next to the kilo’s. The toolbox had a masterlock on it, Naheem asked, “Where the key for this shit?”

“It's in the tank.” Sean nodded his head towards the 150 gallon fish tank in the living room.

Naheem walked over to the tank and looked at it as if he were admiring the fish.

“Where at in the tank?”

“It's under the gravel on the right hand side closest to the wall.”

Naheem rolled up his sleeve and dug into the tank moving the black and red gravel around. Seconds later a small key peaked from under the gravel. Naheem grabbed it and walked back into the dining room. He kneeled in front of the tool box and inserted the key, as he turned it the lock popped. Naheem lifted the top off the toolbox and looked inside before he began to pull kilo's out placing them on the carpet next to the other kilo's. Naheem pulled eight kilo's in all from the toolbox and a .380 Smith-n-Wesson. Hook looked from the eight kilo's on the ground to Sean.

“Awight, Bigboy, where that cash at?”

“All my money in a bank in Atlanta, I got little over a

mill in my house down there."

Naheem calmly walked over to Sean and leveled the triangle barrel of the Desert Eagle to his forehead.

"Look Big boy, you bullshittin us. Just give us the fuckin money and we gone. If I have to ask you again you won't make it to see the next five minutes. Tell us where it's at because if I have to search and I find it you ain't gon have to worry about spending that change you got down the "A".

Sean just stared at Naheem for a minute then he turned to Hook, "Why it gotta be like this Hook?"

Hook curled his reefer-stained lips, "Man look, I'm fucked up. I really need this bread. Once I get it I'm gone, we leavin town. Don't die over no paper yo. You got cash down the "A" to spend."

Sean thought about Hooks words for minute.

"Check the bathroom vent."

In no time Naheem was up the stairs and in the bathroom. The vent was on the floor. Naheem removed the metal grill that covered it and stuck his hand straight down feeling nothing. He looked down in the vent and noticed that about five inches from the opening was a duct that ran into the main vent. Naheem stuck his hand in the duct and pulled out a stack of hundred dollar bills. He continued pulling until he couldn't feel any money left in the duct. Naheem looked down at the money on the floor and wondered how much it was. He picked it up and returned to the dining room and placed the stacks of neatly wrapped hundred dollar bills amongst the cocaine on the floor.

"Man that's everything," Sean said, looking depressed.

Naheem smiled.

“Yeah, you did good Big boy. Let me put all this shit up and Ima let you go.”

Naheem retrieved the duffle bag. He began filling it with all the contents on the floor except for the one kilo he placed on the table in front of Sean.

“That's for your time my nig.” Naheem said with a grin. Hook turned to Naheem.

“I think we should leave out the back way.”

“Awight.”

Naheem unlocked and slid the patio door open slightly then told Sean, “Awight Big boy, this where we go our separate ways. Ima cut that tape off you and we all gon bounce, you got that?”

Sean eagerly shook his head up and down. He had it in his mind that as soon as he got loose he would see to it that Naheem and Hook died painful deaths.

Right now he just had to play his cards right. Naheem went to the kitchen and returned with a steak knife. First he cut Sean's legs free and put the duct tape in his pocket before he moved around to the back of the chair to cut his hands loose. Naheem told Sean to stay seated while he put the knife in the bag. Naheem looked at Hook who was standing to the left of Sean with his gun aimed at his head. Naheem gave him a slight head nod.

“Booom!”

Hooks small cannon roared. A .45 slug slammed into the left side of Seans head with deadly force and his brains exploded out the right side of his face.

Sean was dead on impact but in shock, the blast caused

him to stand then fall to the carpet. Hook ran out the back patio followed by Naheem. They ran down behind the townhouses in darkness until they reached McClean. They stop running and walked across the street. Naheem told Hook, "Meet me at the safehouse."

Hook nodded getting inside his car. Naheem kept walking past the gas station until he got to his car in the shopping center parking lot. He threw the duffle bag on the passenger seat and pulled off.

* * * * * * *

It took Naheem twenty minutes to get to the safehouse. Hook had been sitting in the parking lot only a few minutes before he saw Naheem's car turn in the complex and park. Naheem got out with duffle bag in hand and walked towards the apartment building where he was met by a smiling Hook.

"What I tell you? Straight money!"

"You know what you know."

Naheem smiled and punched his code in the keypad. Inside the apartment Naheem and Hook sat on the lounge chair. Naheem began to take everything out the duffle bag placing the items on the table in front of them. The 27 kilo's sat in one pile with the stacks of money in another pile beside the .380 and the High Point 9mm Hook took from Sean. Naheem took the cut pieces of tape out his pocket and put it in the duffle bag with the empty tool box and steak knife. Naheem then looked at Hook.

"Break it down."

Hook reached over the table and grabbed kilos of cocaine one by one throwing them in the duffle bag. He took 14 kilo's leaving Naheem with 13. Naheem had begun counting the money placing it in stacks.

"How much in that stack?" Hook asked.

"Ten a stack."

Hook began counting out ten thousand dollar stacks with Naheem. When they were done they had 25 stacks on the table, all ten thousand a piece. Hook picked up one and gave Naheem five thousand.

"Grab 12."

Naheem randomly chose 12 stacks placing it in a pile on the far end of the table. The remaining 12 stacks Hook put in the duffle bag. Hook turned to Naheem with a puzzled look on his face.

"Yo... how you know that nigga had more shit in there?" Naheem smiled.

"He gave the shit up too easy, that let me know he had more. He just tried to give us something to satisfy us with. I think it was more in there but fuck it." Naheem paused for a second.

"Look yo, Ima need you later." Then he went on to give Hook a brief summary of the shooting out Brooklyn and the news of Tavon and his murder for hire plot.

"You already fuckin know, hit me when you need me my nig." Hook said as he stood and put the .380 and the 9mm in the duffle bag.

Naheem went to the kitchen and came back with a brown paper bag and put the $125,000 inside.

"Hold up, we gon leave at the same time." He told

Hook.

Naheem sat the paper bag containing the money on the table while he stacked 7 kilo's and took them into the kitchen and put them in one of the empty cabinets. He did the same with the other six and was ready to go.

"Awight, let's bounce."

Naheem grabbed the paper bag off the table and headed for the door with Hook behind him holding the duffle bag. As Naheem grabbed the door knob he turned to Hook.

"Make sure you get rid of everything."

Hook just nodded his head as they both left the apartment. In the parking lot they got in their cars and went their separate ways.

* * * * * * *

It was 2:20 in the morning when Naheem arrived home. When he reached the bedroom everything was just how he left it and Netta was still sleeping peacefully. He went over to the walk in closet and put the .44 back in the Christian Louboutin shoe box. Naheem looked around the closet for somewhere to put the money that was in the paper bag. He bent over moving shoe boxes around until he found one of Netta's empty tennis shoe boxes. Naheem took the money out of the paper bag and put it in the shoe box, then he reached to the shelf overhead and got the backpack he put there earlier. Naheem neatly placed as much money as he could in the shoe box, then it was placed under the rest of the shoe boxes in the back of the closet. Money was still left in the backpack that couldn't fit in the shoe box so

Naheem zipped the backpack and placed it back on the overhead shelf. He then walked into the bedroom, took his clothes off and quietly climbed back in bed beside Netta and fell asleep.

CHAPTER 5

Naheem awoke and found that Netta was gone. He sat up in bed just as she walked back into the bedroom and said, "What time is it?"

"It's almost 8 O'clock."

"Why you up so early?" Naheem quizzed.

Netta sat on the side of the bed.

"I gotta take Prince some clothes to your grandmother's house."

Naheem cut in, "He stayed over there?"

"You know how that boy is about his Na-Na." Turning a bit serious Netta said, "Baby, we need to talk."

"About what?"

"About you, about Prince, about us and our future." Netta was looking directly into Naheem's eyes.

"When is enough enough? Every time you leave I worry about you. You know how I feel about you running around in the streets, you know I lost my brother to the streets. I need you with me... Prince needs his father. What do you think you can do for him dead or locked away for life?"

Naheem had heard this getting out the streets lecture several times before. By now he knew to just sit and listen.

"Naheem, you're driving me crazy, I love you to death. I would lose my mind if something happened to you."

Tears started to fill Netta's eye's and Naheem finally spoke, "Look Cupcake you trippin about nothin. Ain't shit gon happen to me and I ain't goin nowhere. Let me tie up a few loose ends and put some shit in perspective and I'm done, I promise."

"When Naheem? When will this happen... Next year." Tears streamed down Netta's face.

"Give me until Monday. Monday I'll wash my hands of everything I promise. Stop crying." He told her as he wiped her tears away and kissed her on her forehead. She looked in his eyes and smiled a soft smile.

"I love you baby."

"I love you more Cupcake. Look, I need you to check around and see if you can find a good franchise lawyer. Get with one and pick two franchise's that's good to invest in. Tell him you'll get a loan from the bank."

"Which two to pick?"

"He should have a list to choose from. Just pick any two that's profitable and that you won't mind running."

"Okay baby, I'll look on the internet when I get to your grandmother's house."

Netta rose up off the bed. Naheem called out to her as she left the bedroom.

"Ima come in early tonight so we can talk more."

"Okay." She said looking over her shoulder.

Naheem got out the bed and walked to the bathroom. He washed his face and brushed his teeth. When he was done he continued to look at himself in the mirror as he replayed the conversation he and Netta just had. Naheem's thoughts switched to Prince. The last thing Naheem ever wanted was to be a failure in Prince's eyes. He figured if he ended up dead or in jail that meant he failed. He felt his face with both hands as he looked in the mirror and let out a light sigh. He realized that he had a lot of weight on his shoulders and the decisions that he made affected not only himself but those around him also. Naheem knew what had to be done at this point. He walked out the bathroom to the closet and got his red Balenciaga shoes off the shelf and a pair of General Assembly jeans along with a white Trojan Elite T-shirt. Naheem quickly dressed and headed to the safe house.

* * * * * * *

When Naheem finally arrived at the safe house he found Nasir in the living room watching "City of Gods" on DVD.

"Damn yo, you seen that shit a million times."

"It's either this, Shotta's or Scarface." Nasir responded not taking an eye off the 64 inch screen.

Naheem walked straight to the kitchen and got six kilos of cocaine from the cabinet and walked back in the living room placing them on the coffee table in front of Nasir. Seeing the tightly wrapped kilo's on the table stole Nasir's attention. Naheem went back in the kitchen and returned with the other seven kilo's and placed them on the table also before sitting next to Nasir.

"Ima give you these 13 joints at 15 apiece. You can pay me up front or I'll front you them, how you wanna do it?"

Nasir didn't bother to ask where all the cocaine came from. All he knew was this was a deal he couldn't let get past him.

"I'll give you a hundred today and I'll have the 95 for you in two days."

"Awight."

Naheem pushed the kilo's in front of Nasir. "Make sure you get that shit out of here today."

"I got it." Nasir walked the kilo's back to the cabinet. Then he came back in the living room.

"What we gon do about the little nigga Tavon?"

"He'll get his issue soon. What time we supposed to be

meetin Dutch?"

"Any time, I just have to call him when we on the way."

"Awight, let's go now but don't call him until we get out there."

Naheem went to the safe to get his Ruger. When he came back to the living room Nasir was standing by the door waiting on him.

"You ready?"

"Yeah, let's shake."

They left the apartment and got in Nasir's truck. Nasir started the engine and let the sound of T.I. fill the air then pulled out the parking lot.

* * * * * * *

Nasir was at the intersection of Edmondson and Pulaski when the light turned red. The block was extremely busy, Naheem noticed a young man on the corner to the left in front of a New York Fried Chicken carryout. Addicts roamed the corners in search of their next high while others stood around in half nods indirectly endorsing the product that these corners provided. To the right a younger man between the ages of 20 and 25 was crossing the street pushing a pink baby stroller. Naheem vaguely heard Nasir mention something but his attention was averted when the young man pushing the stroller stopped directly in front of them. The man appeared to be bending over to tend to the baby when Naheem heard three quick shots.

Blocka-Blocka-Blocka...!

The first shot went straight through the driver side window and passenger side. Naheem saw the man standing in front of the New York Fried Chicken holding a huge caliber handgun with both hands taking aim as he released the calculated shots. Naheem and Nasir made attempts to reach for their weapons when Nasir was hit in the shoulder with the second shot. The third shot that hit Nasir came through the door panel hitting him in the outer part of the thigh. Nasir slumped over the armrest.

Everything played out in what seemed like a matter of seconds. Just as Naheem got his Ruger up the young man in front of the truck pulled an AK-47 from the stroller. The man with the AK pulled the trigger and bullets the size of crayons shredded everything in their path. Flashes of fire leaped from the assault rifle extending almost four inches.

Naheem couldn't return fire. One of the AK's bullets came straight through the window and hit him in the chest. The force of the hurling bullet pushed him back in the seat. He fell across the armrest on top of Nasir.

"Aaaaah shit!"

The man with the handgun ceased firing then turned and calmly walked down Pulaski. His accomplice sprayed the truck from left to right, then he begun to move along the passenger side of the truck. Naheem felt as if bullets were slamming into him from every direction. He didn't know if he was dead or alive. The chopping sounds of the AK could still be heard in the background as he replayed the conversation he and Netta shared earlier that morning. Naheem felt a cold sensation all over his body along with the taste of blood in his mouth and thought about Prince.

"Damn shorty, Da-Da lost this one."

The hail of AK bullets stopped. Naheem couldn't move, he just lay there. The truck was riddled with holes. The AK cut through it like a hot knife through butter. Naheem coughed up blood as he heard the faint sounds of police and ambulance sirens then his whole body went limp and everything around him got dark.

"Naheem... Yo Naheem. Get up." Naheem heard Nasir uttering. Naheem jumped up and reached for the Ruger that was still on his lap.

"Huh?"

"Get up we here!"

"Yeah, I'm up."

Naheem realized he'd been dreaming, he felt discombobulated. The dream seemed so real, the people, the sounds and the pain, Naheem had even begun to sweat a little as he felt his chest through his shirt.

"You awight yo?"

"Yeah I'm good, I been up all night. I'm straight though... You call Dutch yet?"

"I just got off the phone with him, he on the way."

Naheem scanned the Moe's Seafood restaurants parking lot looking at the cars and people. Once he was sure of his surroundings he sat back in his seat and waited on Dutch.

Moments later a shiny money green Porsche Cayenne eased into the parking lot. Naheem couldn't see its occupants as the vehicle slowly circled the parking lot. It came to a stop a few spaces from Nasir's truck. Nasir's phone lit up. He moved it to his ear.

"Is that you in the Cayenne?"

"Yeah that's me, Ima come to ya'll." Dutch said. A few moments later Dutch was opening the back door of Nasir's truck.

"I told you the other night, if I had your hand I'd cut both of mine off." Nasir said jokingly as Dutch slid into the back seat of the truck.

Dutch revealed his pearly white teeth in a smile. "You still on joke time."

"Who whip is that ?" Naheem asked.

"That's my cousin shit, the one I told you was in the Air Force. He just came home a couple weeks ago. He a square type nigga but he good though."

"The square's the ones that last." Naheem said. Noticing the look that Nasir gave him Naheem frowned.

"Tell me why I was duckin bullets the other night?"

Naheem shifted in his seat to get a better look at two

young ladies who walked past the front of the truck with bags baring Moe's logo. His eyes followed them as their outfits strained to conceal their bodies. One of the women tried to see the occupants of the truck through the windshield. Her companion said something to her that Naheem couldn't make out then they both laughed as they made their way to a small dark sedan.

"E.J. was fuckin dude girl..." Naheem snapped out of his revelry.

"You tellin me that I'm duckin shots about a piece of pussy?" Naheem turned and looked at Dutch in disbelief.

"Naw yo, it's deeper than that." Dutch said.

"You okay, cause you ain't listening." Nasir interjected. "I hope it is deeper than that." Naheem said.

"E.J. was fuckin yo bitch," continued Dutch, "shorty people is the weed connect, they Jamaicans. When E.J. started fuckin shorty she was wide open and turned him on to her people. They liked E.J.'s turn out more than dudes so they cut him off and started dealin exclusively with E.J. Dude name is Poe, he from Cherry Hill but he got a little spot out Cedonia on Lasalle. E.J. got the address from ole girl but he the soft spot. His cousin name Husky from Belair road is the gun slinga. Him and his team pushin Haze on Belair and Cliftview. They supposed to be the ones who left them bodies in Lake Clifton Park a few weeks ago."

"Yeah, I heard about that." Nasir cut in, "It was a lot of different rumors goin around about them two niggaz that got dumped."

Naheem shifted again in his seat and looked out his window onto the parking lot in thought.

"So, when do you wanna holla at these niggaz?" Asked Dutch.

Naheem thought a second more, then spoke, "I don't want you involved Dutch." Dutch parted his lips to speak.

Naheem raised his hand, "I know they know you E.J. man and if you roll with us it'll fuck up the element of surprise. I'm not into shootouts back and forth. I like to get my point across the first time. I got certified hittaz so tell E.J. I said to heal up and chill, this is my favor to him. All I want is for him to be there if and when I ever need him. A favor for a favor." Dutch smiled.

"Man you already know, that go without saying."

"Good. Can you move coke on your end?"

"I can sell snow to a Eskimo."

Naheem chuckled, "Okay, you'll get a call from Nasir in a day or two." Dutch took his leave and hopped out the truck after a few departing words. Nasir looked at Naheem.

"Where to from here?" He asked as he started the truck and pulled out the parking space.

"Harford Road." Naheem replied as he reached for his phoneandpunchedin number.

CHAPTER 6

After confirming that Hook would be able to get everything he felt he would need, Naheem sat back in the truck to await E.J.'s call. He hoped E.J. wouldn't have a problem getting the address. The sun rose and took its position in the sky. The sky was white with light blue and gold streaks crossing it. On cue, the city started to come alive.

Time to work Naheem thought while staring lethargically at the passing crowds.

Naheem's phone vibrated as Nasir turned onto Gorsuch and parked.

"Tell me some good news." Naheem said into the phone. "Twenty five-0-one." He repeated what E.J. told him, then hung up.

"Yo, you gon tell me why we need that shit you told Hook to get?"

Puzzled, Naheem rubbed the top of his head as it dawned on him that he did not bother to tell Nasir about his dream of them being shot up inside the truck. I might tell him later, Naheem thought, right now we got more pressing shit to think about. Smiling at the irony of the attack, Naheem reached for his doorknob.

“It's time to roll we gotta meet everybody else on Lake Clifton parking lot behind the school.”

As Hook stood in the parking lot talking to his four most trusted soldiers, a black van turned off Saint Lo Drive and headed in their direction. The vehicle stopped near a gray minivan with 3 dirt bikes leaning against it. When it's front doors opened, Naheem and Nasir stepped out of it and walked over to the small army dressed in black Timbs, jeans and hoodies. Giving them their marching orders, Naheem stood in the center of the 7 men. He turned to Nasir first.

“Nai, you drive the van and -,” Nasir contracted his dark eyebrows.

“Hold on, Nah, why I gotta drive the damn van -- Why can’t I --?”

At first Nasir objected to having to be the driver of the black van but soon accepted his role as the best thing for everybody. The three assassin's on the dirt bikes and a minivan would be sent to Poe’s house with clear instructions to be sure they got their man and to put all the weapon’s in the minivan before they left the scene. A phone call with one ring to Nasir's phone would let them know that the mission was successfully completed.

Hook and Naheem would take care of Husky and anybody else that was lurking on the block. The girl they sent to Cliftview to identify Husky name was Boo. She had already called back with Husky's description and said he was hugging the block with two other men. She was then told to do all she could to keep him on the block but to call if he left. Naheem, Hook, and Nasir climbed into the van and headed for Cliftview.

Nasir was told to pull over at Cliftview and Belair and let them out. Hook lifted a stroller from the van as Naheem took out a wheelchair. After helping Naheem adjust himself in the wheelchair Hook handed him a pistol grip Mosberg pump. Naheem briefly admired it's blue steel and rubber grip before he tucked it between his legs. A blanket was thrown over his lap to conceal the weapon. Naheem slipped on his black leather gloves and steered the wheelchair onto Belair Road.

Wasting no time, Hook took a Mac 11 out and placed it under a blanket next to a doll baby and pushed the stroller to its destination. Following his instructions to wait for them at the end of Cliftview. Nasir was seated behind the wheel in a van. He cut off the music and lowered his window to stay alert.

At a break in the traffic, Naheem gripped the tires on his wheelchair. Naheem rolled himself across Belair Road. Playing the cripple part to the max, he slowed down and caused an angry motorist to blow his horn.

"Stupid nigga, get your cripple ass out of the fuckin street!" The driver shouted out of the window of an Escalade.

Naheem had bigger fish to fry so he just smiled and flipped the driver the "fuck you" finger and kept pushing. It pleased Naheem to see that no kids were standing near Husky and that there were only a handful of crackheads attempting to obtain a mid-day fix. Otherwise the block was relatively quiet.

Boo stood near Husky. Naheem had briefed her to be on the lookout for him and when he came to make an excuse to leave. On cue, when she spotted who she was looking for she reached down, grabbed Husky's crotch and leaned over whispering something in his ear that put a lewd grin on his face. As Boo walked away towards the corner store Hook crossed Cliftview to back up Naheem and to shoot anyone who got in his way. Putting more slump into his shoulders after he rolled up on the curve, Naheem made out like he was struggling to move his wheelchair as he eased closer to his target. Husky held a cellphone to his ear grinning and laughing when Naheem came to a stop directly in front of him. Naheem leaned over and rubbed his legs, and then, in one fluid motion he hopped out of the wheelchair with the Mosberg and aimed it at Husky. Husky's eyes morphed to the size of two silver dollars.

"Oh shi --"

The first blast hit him in the shoulder and the cellphone flew out his hand and clattered against the sidewalk. The blast left Husky's right arm dangling from his shoulder by a piece of skin.

"Aaahh!" He managed to scream just before another blast tore a hole in his chest and slammed him against a rowhouse killing him before his body hit the ground.

The crackheads in the area scattered in all directions. A man wearing a hoodie and holding a .45 Glock ran across the street towards Naheem. Naheem's Mosberg was held down by his side. From a distance of about four cars Hook let loose a volley of shots.

'Tat Tat Tat... Tat Tat... Tat Tat Tat Tat...'

Hearing the gunfire, Naheem brought up the pump again as he whirled around in the direction of the shots and saw Hook and the Mac 11 in his hand. The man wearing the hoodie lay out on the ground in a pool of blood. A single look was all it took for Naheem to know he was dead. Winking an eye at Hook, Naheem lowered the pump down by his side again and proceeded down the street away from the crime scene. Before he reached the corner Hook caught up with him. At the end of Cliftview, they hopped into the back of the van. Nasir looked at them over his shoulder and grinned before pulling away.

"Ya'll good?" Hook returned Nasir's smile.

"Soundboy burial."

"Did you get that call?" Naheem asked Nasir.

"Not yet." Nasir said keeping his eye's on the traffic.

"Don't trip, my lil niggas about that drama." Hook said.

Naheem nodded at Hook then leaned back in his seat and fell silent.

Moments later in Cedonia ...

Poe didn't find the young man on the dirt bike popping wheelies up and down his block strange. A lot of parents bought their kids dirt bikes in his neighborhood, that's what lead him to believe it was just another neighborhood kid out having fun. What he did find strange was that his front door was ajar as he pulled into his driveway and put the car in park. Swiveling his head around to back the car out of the driveway, Poe's brown eyes nearly popped out of his long head by the sudden appearance of two more young boys on dirt bikes. Wearing black bandanas, black hoodies and Nike baseball gloves, one of the riders stopped directly behind the Lexus while the other two approached it's driver from the left side. Poe forgot the car was in park. He mashed down on the gas pedal in vain. The engine revved but the Lexus remained in place. The rider behind the car took aim with a huge 40 cal. handgun. Everything moved in slow motion for Poe, the rider's trigger finger, the explosion, the four bullets, the shattering of the rear windshield, the command from Poe's brain to react. The reaction that never came.

Leaving Poe paralyzed and numb, the first bullet fractured his spine. The second slug went through the back of his neck and came out his jugular. Shots three and four crashed into the back of Poe's head blowing chunks of his cheek and forehead off. Poe was already dead when the hail of bullets flew through the driver's window into the side of his face and shoulder. The two gunmen on the driver side emptied their Glocks mercilessly into Poe's body. Poe's last thoughts were splattered over the front interior of his car.

A block and a half from the safehouse, inside the black van Nasir's phone rung once then stopped.

* * * * * * *

30 minutes later in the safehouse Naheem, Nasir and Hook conversated about sports and females while they waited on Nephew to arrive. Hook started fidgeting.

"Damn... Nephew takin long as shit."

Nasir shrugged, "He should be here in a few minutes."

Naheem's phone vibrated. He raised it to his ear.

"Yo."

"What it is? I got that shit from my peoples a little while ago." Kayo said. Naheem smiled.

"That's what's up, ya'll should be straight for a minute."

"Yeah we good, Vailz tryna put the minutes on the phone now."

There was a knock at the door and Nasir got up to check the peephole. He opened the door and Nephew came walking in and exchanged hand clasps around the room. Nephew got to Naheem who was still on the phone with Kayo.

"What it do?" Naheem looked up at Nephew.

"Ain't shit, just waitin on your slow ass."

"That's Nephew?" Kayo asked Naheem.

"Yeah, shorty just walked in."

"Tell'em I said what's up and I send my love." Kayo said.

Naheem relayed the message and Nephew responded, "tell that nigga I love him too and I'll be glad when he come home."

Before Naheem could tell Kayo what Nephew said Kayo blurted, "Yo, they just called me for an attorney visit Ima holla back."

"Awight shorty holla."

Naheem ended the call and stood to stretch his legs. "Nasir, where do you see yourself in five years?"

Nasir was caught off guard. "Umm... I ain't really

thought about it yo. I mean, I don't really know."

Naheem turned to Hook, "what about you?"

"You already know where Ima be my nig, Ima still be getting this money. Ima eat in these streets until one of those bitch ass niggas take me out the game."

Everything he said seemed twisted but somehow made sense to him. Naheem didn't even entertain it. He continued with Nephew.

"Where you see yourself in five years?"

"Man... I really don't know but I got some ideas."

"Like what? What kind of ideas?"

"I wanna get my money right and fuck with some houses... Oh, and I want a shoe store too, like Downtown Locker room. In five years I wanna be like you yo."

"It's too much room to be better than me, that's where you should be aiming at. Them plans you got is good, it ain't hard as you think. This shit ain't goin to be sweet forever. How Nephew the youngest in here and thought more about his future then ya'll?" Naheem shot at Nasir and Hook.

Naheem never thought this day would come, what he felt spoke to his soul. He had mixed emotions about the decision he made. He felt as though he was abandoning his team knowing that they needed him. On the other hand, he was relieved to walk away from it all. His son needed him and in turn he needed Netta. Naheem remembered something that his uncle told him as a child, "Nah, if Allah meant for you to love two things he would've put two hearts in your chest."

"Awight yo, this is what it is. Monday is my last day in

the game."

"What that mean, what we gon do without you?" Nephew asked.

"Damn, give a nigga a chance to finish." Naheem said, then flashed an assuring smile. "After Monday I'm done with everything. I'm leaving the game to Nasir and you will oversee all the shops." Naheem pointed to Nephew who was frowning.

"What's up yo?"

"Man, I feel all that shit but it ain't gon be the same without you."

"Nigga you act like Ima be dead or something, I ain't goin nowhere. I'm moving out the streets to do some bigger better shit. This is your time to get your bread up and do all that shit you just said you wanted to do. You got age and time on your side. This shit don't last forever so Ima quit while I'm ahead ya dig." Nephew didn't speak but he nodded his head.

"Just the other day you was talkin about promotions, now it's your time to be the man you nuttin up on me." Naheem said teasing Nephew who was now smiling.

Naheem's phone vibrated. The screen indicated that he had a text message. A simple X from X. Naheem put the phone back in his pocket.

"Awight look, this is over for now but we'll put everything together later."

Naheem turned to Nasir, "Ima holla at Roberto. I need you to get that change you owe me to Prinshe, she should be at the boutique. Tell her Ima holla at her when I'm done."

“Damn yo, when you gon give shorty a word for me?” Nasir quizzed.

“I keep tellin you, me and shorty grew up together and I ain’t never seen her fuck with a nigga in the streets. She ain't gon listen to me anyway, ask Hook.” Naheem gestured in Hooks direction. Hook looked up from a Don Diva magazine he was thumbing through.

“He ain't neva lied, I been chasin shorty forever, I gave up. Now her sexy ass got that boutique she all on her grind so you really ain't got shit coming.”

“I’m goin with you.” Nephew said to Nasir.

“Good cause I wanted to holla at you more about your new position.” Hook closed the Don Diva and sat it on the table.

“Fuck it, I'm goin too. I ain’t doin shit.”

Nasir grabbed his cell phone off the table. “Awight, let's bounce.”

“Awight ya’ll.” Naheem said to the trio. “Nephew.”

At the door, Nephew stopped and turned. “Yeah.”

“When I'm done Ima call you.”

“Awight.”

CHAPTER 7

While Naheem drove to little Italy to meet Roberto, he mulled over his past in hopes of finding answers. He thought about how happy he was when his mother was alive. As a child his mother gave him a sense of protection and she would smile when he brought home various certificates from school. For a kid in the inner city she sheltered him from a lot of the ill's that plagued the streets.

Most of all, she instilled in him what it meant to be a man. *One day when Young and his mother walked to a bus stop, she told him, "When you walk with a lady you always walk on the curbside of the street."*

Young Naheem was inquisitive. "Mommy... Why do a man gotta walk by the street?"

His mother looked down at him. "You suppose to always protect a lady. The man walk on the street side because if a car jump the curb you can protect the lady."

Naheem walked around his mother to the street side and held her hand. Naheem always smiled when he reminisced that day. "Those were good times," he thought as he went down North Ave., but short lived. Naheem's mother had a secret that she kept from him and it ate her alive.

"This is it." She decided one day. "I got to tell my baby."

She walked into Naheems room, her pride and joy was watching movies. Naheem had just turned eight.

"Naheem... Let's talk for a minute." His mother cut off the television.

"Okay mommy." Young Naheem said with a smile.

"Naheem, you know I love you right." Naheem shook his head up and down.

"Well... Naheem... Mommy is H.I.V. positive, do you know what H.I.V. is?"

"Hmm-mmm." Naheem said shaking his head from side to side.

"It's a disease that doesn't have a cure. See... what it really means is mommy has to watch her health and what she eats because now little things like a small cold could hurt."

Naheem sat and listened to his mother trying to make him understand the severity of H.I.V. Still not fully comprehending the ramifications of H.I.V., young Naheem jumped up and ran out the room.

"Naheem!" His mother called out after him.

Young Naheem returned moments later with a bottle of Flintstone vitamins. "Take these mommy! They make me feel better."

Naheem put the bottle of vitamins in his mother's hand. As honest as Naheems actions were, he had no idea that he was making the situation that much more perplex for his mother. She took the bottle of vitamins from him and sat them down.

"No baby, it's not that easy. H.I.V. can't be fixed right now but doctors are working on trying to fix it."

Young Naheem just sat there, to him this didn't make sense. The vitamins always made him feel better. "Why don't they work now?" He thought. He couldn't fathom the thought of his mother being sick and not getting better. Young Naheem looked his mother in the eye's.

"Do that mean you gon die mommy?"

"No baby, I'm not going anywhere, I'm going to be fine." She kissed him on the forehead and hugged him tight.

* * * * * * *

Naheem drove silently down Broadway towards Little Italy which was located in the Fells Point area of Baltimore. Years ago Little Italy had been predominantly occupied by Italians. All in the 5O's, 60's, 70's and early 8O's Little Italy had been the hub and headquarters for the Italian Mafia. In recent years Little Italy had gotten an influx of South American immigrants.

Once Naheem crossed Eastern Ave. both sides of Broadway bloomed with bars, restaurants and clubs. Fells Point was a multicultural environment and being as though it sat at the edge of Baltimore's Inner Harbor, Fells Point also served as a tourist attraction. Because the day was still young, the presence of people was moderate. Naheem parked on a small side street and got out. Walking back on Broadway, he smelt various herbs and spices that the summer's breeze carried. He strolled into an establishment that read Jose's Bar and Grill in lights mounted on the front of the red brick building. Soft music came from hidden speakers. As many times as he had been to Jose's Bar and Grill, it always seemed as if it was his first time visiting.

The dining room was in the front of the restaurant, the bar in back. Naheem savored the warmth of the Mediterranean style decor, the music, the aroma and the fireplaces. At the bar Naheem spotted Roberto conversing with Gia, one of the two barmaids. Gia spoke as Naheem approached.

"Hi Senor Naheem." Roberto turned on his bar stool and extended his hand.

"How are you my friend?"

"Hey Gia. I'm fine Roberto." Naheem smiled as he shook Roberto's hand.

Gia returned the smile and walked down the bar to take someone's order. Roberto was of Mexican descent. He was neatly dressed as usual. He sported a cream Armani linen shirt and pant set with a simple but pricey Patek Philippe watch on his left wrist and a pair of Armani loafers. Roberto's jet black hair was combed to the back. The Emporio Armani Meccanico sunglasses which sat on his tanned face hid his eyes.

"Would you like anything?" Roberto offered.

"Yeah, I'll have a Goose and cranberry." Naheem mounted the bar stool next to Roberto.

Roberto waved to the other barmaid Kania. Gia and Kania were cousins although they looked so much alike they could pass for sisters. Kania walked past Naheem, as she waved to him he gave her a light smile and waved back. Kania stood in front of Roberto and spoke rapid Spanish.

“Si Senor quieres tomar algo?”

“Si, me qustaria aqua elada y mi amigo Jugo de uva con fresa de Hielo.”

“Eso va a ser todo Senor?”

“Si grasias.” Roberto said before Kania turned and walked away. Roberto then turned back to Naheem.

“How has everything been Naheem?”

“Everything is fine man but --” Naheem felt his phone vibrating, when he looked at the screen Kayo's code popped up so he sent the call to his voicemail and continued.

“Everything's fine. I need to talk to you about some new arrangements.”

“Oh, new arrangements you say... What new arrangements would that be?” Roberto removed his sunglasses and placed them on the bar.

“Roberto man, I'm done. I want out yo.”

“What's the matter Senor, are you not pleased with my product?”

Naheem let out a light chuckle. Roberto asked, “What's funny Senor?”

“Man, the product... the product couldn't be any better. This town ain't seen no smack that can stand on a twenty since the 80's. The product is definitely not the problem.” Naheem assured him.

“Then where is the problem Senor?”

“There is no problem. Shit couldn't be better. I'm just tired, I got a son to raise and enough money to see that his future is bright. I see people all the time that grind hard and don't even get a chance to enjoy what they worked so hard for... Either they get killed or the Feds take it. I'm ahead of the game and I'm ready to cash in my chips."

"Since you put it that way my friend, I understand. Is it anything I can do for you?"

Before Naheem could answer Kania returned and placed coasters in front of them, then she put Naheem's drink on the coaster and placed a glass of ice water in front of Roberto. When she was done Roberto nodded his head and Kania was off again.

Naheem continued, "I'm good... I'm good I just want my man to take my spot."

Roberto looked at Naheem for a second, "My friend, my business relationship is with you."

"I understand that but I trust this guy. He's goin to be running the show I just need you to back him."

Roberto put his sunglasses back on his face, took a sip of the ice water then turned to Naheem.

"My friend, in my country we have a saying. Loyalty and honor, like gold and diamonds, owe's it's value only to its scarcity."

Naheem was silent taking it all in when finally Roberto pulled an ink pen from his pocket and sat it on the bar. He then pushed the ink pen along with a napkin to Naheem.

"Write his full name on here."

Naheem did as he was told and slid the ink pen and napkin back. Roberto glanced at the name on the napkin before he balled it up, placed it in an ashtray on the bar and set it on fire.

“Text me your friends social security number, then never use that number again.”

“Roberto wrote a few digits on another napkin and slid it to Naheem. “If... your friend is clean this will be the number for him to contact me. I assume that you'll prep him?”

“He gon do everything how he supposed to.” Naheem assured Roberto. “Start him with ten boys and twenty girls and he’ll go from there. He should only need you once a month. I'll walk him through the first deal all the way up to showing him how to mail the money, then he on his own.”

“I see my friend, you'll know if he checks out tomorrow.”

Roberto wrote a figure on another napkin and slid it to Naheem. He looked at it and nodded his head. Roberto pulled the napkin back, balled it up, placed it in the ashtray and set it on fire.

“If your friend is clean that's what we agree on.” Roberto extended his hand.

Naheem happily shook Roberto's hand. “Agreed.”

“So my friend, do you have any retirement plans.”

“Naw not really. I just wanna be with my family. I think Ima ask my girl to marry me. She been loyal since day one, she deserve it.”

“Ah ha my friend, allow me to loan you Princesa Estrella as a small token of my appreciation.” Roberto smiled at Naheem.

“What's that?”

“It's my yacht, it means Princess Starr in English. Starr is my god daughter in La Tuna de Badiraquato, because I have no kids I name my boat after her. I'll have Gia or Kania alert my staff of your coming. It's stocked with Armand de Brignac (Ace of Spade) and whatever the chef doesn't have on board he'll dock to get it for you."

"That sound nice man but I can't--"

"My friend, you've been of good service to me. Accept my offer." Naheem broke a smile.

"Awight... Where do I have to go?"

"The Princesa Estrella is docked in the Harbor my friend. You can board her from the main Harbor or the Canton dock on the other side of the Harbor."

"I'd like to get on at the main Harbor so I can park in the parking garage."

"The main Harbor it is my friend. She'll be there in 45 minutes if you would like to meet the staff ahead of time. Have fun, you got her for as long as you like."

"I'm kinda busy today but I'll check with the staff tomorrow."

"That's fine my friend, take your time."

"Thanks man, that means alot to me." Naheem told Roberto.

"No problem my friend, if you ever need me I'm here. Gia and Kania always know how to contact me." Roberto winked his left eye. Naheem saw it move through the slight tint. Naheem finished his drink in one gulp then stepped down off the bar stool.

"I got some things to handle Roberto, Ima holla later."

"Our business here is done my friend." Roberto affirmed with an outstretched hand.

After shaking Roberto's hand Naheem turned and

walked out of Jose's Bar and Grill. Once Naheem got to his car he sat there for a second. "The hard part is done," he thought.

* * * * * * *

While driving to meet Prinshe, Naheem slipped back to his childhood. *At 12 he had all the signs of a promising future. His mother had been hospitalized for a bad case of bronchitis which took a great toll on her due to her H.I.V. infection.*

This day would be the first in weeks that Naheem would get to see her due to all the surgeries that she had to undergo and the doctors limiting her visits. Naheem couldn't wait to see his mother. Nothing on the face of the earth could make him feel the way he did when she smiled at him. He had a lot to tell her and he wanted her home. Young Naheem walked to Mercy Hospital with all smiles. When he walked into his mother's room she was sleeping peacefully. He was so excited he had to wake her up.

"Mommy... mommy wake up." He said as he stood beside the bed.

Her eyes slowly opened and focused in on him. She gave him a weak smile, almost as if it hurt.

"Mommy, you okay?"

"Yeah... I'm alright... baby." She slurred in a near whisper.

At that moment Naheem noticed that his mother's once bright eyes were dim and her face looked as if she'd lost some weight.

"Mommy... Why you sound like that?" Young Naheem asked as he took a seat on the side of the bed.

"I got a little fluid on the brain baby but don't worry about me. How you been?"

By now Naheem had his head on her stomach with his arms around her. In a weak voice and slurred tone she said, "Baby what's wrong, you okay?"

Naheem didn't answer. His mother then began to rub his back when she heard light sobs and felt him squeeze her tighter.

"Naheem... Why are you crying?."

At that point, Naheem couldn't hold it in any longer. He heaved and sobbed.

"You gon die, I don't want you to go."

"Naheem... Naheem stop, I'm not going anywhere. Come pray with me." She wiped tears from his face.

Naheem got up and they held hands as he repeated a short prayer after her. They sat and talked until the visit was over. Naheem gave his mother a hug and kiss then left.

A few weeks later Naheem was at his grandmother's house when she told him, "Naheem guess what, your mother's home." Naheem was elated, his mother was finally home.

"Can you take me home grandma." The excited Naheem asked.

"Yeah, get your clothes and come on."

Naheem's grandmother drove him home. The front door was wide open. He ran past several family members that stood around and watched as young Naheem made his way over to his mother who was sleeping in her bed. Naheem knew she would not only be happy to be home but she would be happy to see him as well. He just wanted to tell her that he loved her and that she was home because they had prayed.

"Mommy... mommy wake up." Naheem anticipated seeing the glow in her eyes.

"Mommy, get up."

Young Naheem heard sniffles and weeping coming from various family members.

He reached down to put his hands on her shoulders and gave her a light shake. "Mommy, get up."

The sobs in the background turned into loud cry's. Naheem violently began to shake his mother's lifeless body, at this point he was hysterical and was now screaming.

"Mommy wake up... wake up... we prayed... you told me you wasn't gon die!"

Tears ran down young Naheem's face, he was frantic. He hadn't even realized how hard he was shaking his mother's body. Naheem was in shock. Someone grabbed him from the back.

"She gone man, she gone."

"No... she not! She sleep!"

Naheem never turned to see who had grabbed him, he tried to fight his way back to his mother as she lay motionless.

At the funeral young Naheem sat in the front row and had a clear view of his mother in her casket. Sobs could be heard throughout the entire church. Naheem was still in shock, he was mentally distraught. He hadn't ate anything in days. The full meaning of his mother's death hadn't set in. With all the events that took place, young Naheem didn't understand why everybody was so sad. He knew his mother was going to wake up and get out that casket and smile at him.

"She wouldn't lie to me," he thought.

Now, many years later, as Naheem pulled up on Light Street and parked, a few tears ran down his brown cheeks. He used the back of his hand to dry his face but the pain he felt in his heart was still there. He wished he could somehow wipe the pain away that easy.

"Time does heal wounds but what about the scars," he thought as he pulled himself together and exited the car.

CHAPTER 8

Naheem walked down Light Street until he was in front of a building that read Shay's Boutique on a pink awning. The front window was adorn with all sorts of Stilletto platform and high heel shoes. When Naheem entered the boutique he noticed that the floor workers were busy tending to the growing multitude of consumers. Naheem maneuvered through the small mob and was greeted by the cashier.

"Hey Naheem."

"What's up Brittany. Where Shay at?"

"She's back in her office, hold on, let me tell her you're out here."

Brittany picked up the phone that sat to the left of the cash register and dialed the extension to Prinshe's office. After a few words Brittany hung up.

"Naheem, she said she want to talk to you in her office."

"Awight, thanks."

Naheem walked through a door and down a short hallway. Two lipstick cameras sat above the door on both ends of the corridor, they were so small that Naheem knew they were there and still couldn't see them. When he reached the red oak door at the end of the hallway, he could hear Prinshe's voice over the intercom.

"It's open."

Naheem opened the door and saw Prinshe sitting behind a huge red oak desk.

When he entered she got up and met him in the middle of the office. They embraced and she gave him a light peck on the lips.

"How you been?"

"I'm good, you get that from Nasir?"

"Yeah, I got it, it was $125,000. Naheem, I think you need to get a broker. I can only do but so much. Even though the boutique is doing good, I can't explain almost $500,000 in one week, and that don't include what the boutique really made. Too much money is detectable, it's easy to trace."

"Awight, Do this for right now... keep 25, put 25 in Prince's account, put another 25 in a Treasury Bond for five years and put the rest in CD's for two years. We'll look for a broker in a few days."

"Okay, I'll have the money in Prince's account by Friday. I donated the last money you gave me to that list of non-profit organizations like you told me to. I'll write it off on my taxes. When I get my tax returns where do you want me to put it?"

"I ain't sure yet, Netta lookin into a few franchises so when she finish that part I'll let you know." Naheem explained. "You really need to be lookin for more locations so we can expand."

Prinshe picked up a pen and twirled it in her fingers.

"I talked to KeKe and she said she can get us a nice store in DC. I told her I wanted to get in Georgetown, she said it would be hard but she would try to pull some strings."

"That's good, when she supposed to be getting back at you?"

"By the end of the week. Business been so good I hardly have time to do anything. I designed three new pair of stiletto's." She pushed Naheem pictures of the shoes across her desk. Naheem looked at the pictures and was impressed.

"I like these." Prinshe smiled at his approval.

"We have to expand, I think it's time to take our show on the road." He said still looking at the pictures. He felt his phone vibrate.

"Yeah what's up." Naheem said into the phone.

"I was just makin sure you was straight, you ain't neva hit me." Nasir said relieved to hear from Naheem.

"Damn yo, I got caught up and forgot."

"I gave your peoples an extra quarter too."

"Yeah she good." Naheem responded not wanting to say much over the phone. "I got some good news for you. We gon be at the house waitin on you."

"That's what's up. I'll be there in a few. Aye yo... I almost forgot, text me your social security number so I can put it on that job application."

"Awight." Nasir said before disconnecting the call.

Prinshe was sorting through a pile of paperwork that sat on her desk when Naheem blurt out, "Ima propose to

Netta."

"What! Boy it's about time!"

Prinshe was so excited she ran from around her desk and gave Naheem a big hug and assaulted him with numerous questions before he could even answer the first one.

"Damn yo, one at a time."

"Okay... Did you get her ring yet?"

"Naw, not yet. I really don't know too much about engagement rings. Now I think about it, I don't know shit about weddings period."

"That's what lil sis is for. Let me plan everything, from the wedding to the honeymoon."

"You gotta make my shit a royal event." Naheem joked.

"Is that the green light to go all out?"

"You already know."

"Let's go look at some rings real quick. We can go to that new jewelry store across the street." Prinshe retrieved her clutch purse from the desk drawer.

"Awight."

Naheem's phone vibrated. He looked at it to see that he had a text message from Nasir. He opened the message sent it to Roberto and deleted the old number as Roberto instructed.

Prinshe walked out of her office with Naheem in step behind her. They reached the front of the boutique where a massive crowd had accumulated. Brittany was at the cash register ringing up shoes while the two floor workers hastened to tend to the assembly of patrons. Prinshe walked over to the counter that separated her and Brittany.

"I'll be right back, I'm going across the street."

"Okay." Brittany responded while handing a lady her receipt.

Naheem and Prinshe walked out the boutique and towards Black Pearl's Jewelry Galleria. The Jewelry Galleria sat directly on the corner across the street from Shay's Boutique. When they walked in Black Pearls they approached the counter. The cashier behind the counter spoke in a good natured tone.

"Hi, welcome to Black Pearls Jewelry Galleria. My name is Netra, can I help you?" Prinshe gladly spoke.

"Hi, we would like to look at a few engagement rings."

"Congratulations!" Naheem and Prinshe swiftly looked at each other then back to Netra.

"Uugghh..." Prinshe said while Naheem spoke for the first time.

"Whoa, this like my sister. She just helpin me pick something out."

"Oh, I'm sorry." Netra said. Still a little embarrassed by the small mishap Netra continued her sales pitch. "We're an authorized dealer of several brand names. We carry brands such as Tiffany, Van Cleef & Arpels and Coffin & Trout. A shipment of Venus Diamonds just came in yesterday. Are you looking for anything in particular?"

"Naw, I just want to look at a few." Naheem answered.

"Okay sir, let's see..." Netra directed them to a glass case full of rings. "We'll start at this case and work our way down, just point to the ones you like."

Naheem nodded his head and looked down into the glass case Netra stood in front of.

"This one happens to be one of my personal favorites."

Netra said pointing to one ring.

“That is nice.” Prinshe countered as Netra continued.

“This is a 14 carat white gold engagement ring. It's set with a carat center diamond accented by two round side diamonds totaling.04 carats. It's priced at $550.

“What about this one?” Naheem pointed to a ring in the case next to the one where Netra stood. Netra walked over to the case and opened it removing the ring.

“This is a 10 carat white gold engagement ring. It has, as you can see a graceful swirl design and is set with a round diamond accented by 14 side diamonds totaling .84 carats. It's priced at $1,415.” Netra said as she looked at the little price tag that hung from the ring. Prinshe frowned and shook her head.

“I don't like the design on that one.”

“What about that one right there?” Naheem pointed to a ring in the same case. Netra placed the ring back in its box in the case and removed the ring of Naheem's interest.

“I like that, it's sooo cute.” Prinshe approved with a smile.

“This one is nice. It has a white gold band and features a .67 carat Special Venus quality diamond. The diamond is secure with six prongs and has a 14 carat white gold mounting. This little beauty runs at $3,175.” Prinshe looked at Naheem.

“That is it. That one right there.”

“It's cool but you said it was cute when you saw it, I ain't lookin for cute.”

Naheem then began to scan the glass cases until he saw something that caught his eye.

"That one right there, what's up with that?" Naheem directed Netra and Prinshe's attention to the glass receptacle on their right side. Prinshe's eyes popped.

"Daayyyuumm." Naheem smiled.

"That... is a long way from cute." Netra reached in the glass receptacle and pulled the ring out.

"This little baby here is a platinum diamond engagement ring with a double Venus 1.55 carat round diamond set in a classic four prong setting. It has VVS2 clarity, H color and includes a G.I.A. diamond grading report."

"What G.I.A. mean?" Quizzed Naheem.

"It stands for Gemological Institute if America. It proves the stone is natural and describes any treatments done to it." Netra explained as she went to place the ring back in its case.

The sun beamed through the window. When Netra moved the ring, the light made it sparkle like a disco ball. Naheem thought the diamond winked at him.

"I want that one."

"I think we should go back to the last case sir." Netra expressed not bothering to quote the price.

"You don't get paid to think sweetie." Prinshe said. "How much is the ring?"

"It's $15,325." Netra replied. Prinshe handed Netra her Platinum American Express card along with a business card.

"Charge it. And since your such a great thinker, if things don't work out for you here, you can come work for me."

Naheem remained silent with a sly grin on his face. Netra looked down at the business card in her hand.

"You own Shay's Boutique? I looove your shoes, look I'm wearing a pair now!"

Netra moved from behind the glass receptacles.

Prinshe said, "That's nice sweetie but I need you to bag the ring please, thank you."

Naheem finally spoke to alleviate the situation. Even though Netra deserved it, Prinshe hadn't shown any signs of letting up.

"Can you engrave something on the inside of the band?"

"Yes sir." Netra said clearly glad that he intervened.

"Awight, put Loyalty Is Everything on the inside.

Netra took the ring in the back and returned to the cash register to swipe the credit card. She handed Prinshe a receipt and advised her that the ring wouldn't be ready until tomorrow then tried to explain herself.

"I didn't mean any harm, I just thought... I mean, the ring is really expensive that's all."

"Don't worry yourself honey." Prinshe placed her credit card back in her purse, then she turned and walked away. Outside of Black Pearls Jewelry Galleria Naheem grinned at Prinshe.

"That's why I don't like takin you nowhere. You don't know how to behave."

"Boy, shut up!"

"How about that ring, what you think?"

"She's gonna love it. When are you going to propose?"

"Tomorrow. A friend of mine let me use his yacht."

"That sounds like it's going to be nice." They stood by his car.

"Ima bring you $15,000 tomorrow when I come get the

ring, just hit me when you pick it up."

Naheem leaned over and gave Prinshe a light peck on the forehead before he jumped in the car a drove off.

CHAPTER 9

Naheem returned to the safe house to find Nasir, Hook, and Nephew watching Boyz In The Hood. When he walked in Nasir cut the TV off.

"Man, I got some news for you!"

"What it is?"

"First, I know where the nigga Tavon be. We stopped at the gas station on North and Aisquith and just when I was about to get out, I see's the nigga Tavon across the street at the Quickie Mart. It look like he was over there hustlin. I sent Nephew over there and he say the nigga over there sellin Haze."

"Awight... We gon holla at him in a minute."

"Naw, we gon holla at the nigga. You gon stay here, I got this," Nephew said, "I can get up on the nigga, ain't nobody gon pay me no mind." Hook looked at Naheem.

"Nephew right yo." Naheem nodded.

"Awight, get it in then."

Nasir fingered his chin, then proceeded, "That's the first thing, now the second is we went to meet Hook man Bonez up Park Heights and he lookin for a plug on the girl. I told him I'll meet him tonight, he tryna get two joints. I told him the ticket was $26,500 apiece. I'll have that $53,000 plus the other 17 I owe tomorrow."

"That's what's up. I got with Roberto so tomorrow we should be straight. I told him Ima walk you through the first deal and show you how to mail the money then you on your own. The first shipment is 10 boys and 20 girls, your bill is $850,000. I got the number for you to reach him but I ain't gon give it to you until tomorrow."

Nasir listened to Naheem run everything down. When he was told the price of the first shipment he started to doubt himself.

"850! That's a big bill. I really don't need all that."

Naheem became infuriated. He stormed up to Nasir and stood four inches away from his face. Staring deep into his soul, he spoke to him through gritted teeth.

"Nigga what you mean? I went down there and co-signed for you! Do you know that if you fuck this up you could get me, you and our families killed. This ain't no fuckin game. I put you in position because I trust you to see that shit stay right. Polo turned me on to Roberto and for five years our business been A-1. I expect you to keep it up."

Nasir knew Naheem meant well. But the pressure of owing someone almost a million dollars on the first deal made him hesitant. This was his chance and he knew he wouldn't let him down.

"I got this, don't even trip."

Naheem grinned and slapped Nasir on the shoulder. "That's what I'm talkin about. This shit ain't hard."

“Let's ride out.” Hook said anxious to quench his thirst for blood. Nephew was eager also.

“I'm tryna crush this nigga.” Hook turned to Nephew. “You strapped?”

Nephew adjusted the Glock 19 that he had in his waistband. “Yes Siiirr!”

“Let's move.” Nasir announced then turned to Naheem. “We’ll be right back.”

“Awight, I'll be here.”

The young urban militia left with their minds set on nothing but murder. Naheem took a seat. Not bothering to cut the TV on, he sat there while allowing the silence to massage his brain in an effort to work out the tension. A lot came with growing up in the home of Anthony Jones with a Wille Adams for an idol or a Rudy Williams as a mentor. Baltimore bred a type of individual that couldn't be found anywhere on earth. True, everywhere had ghettos and poverty but none like what plague this city. This city was a city nicknamed by its locals Vietnam because of its ability to mold little boys into cold blooded murders by the tender age of 12, robbing them of not only their innocence but their childhood as well. Heroin being the drug of choice only fueled the fire that was burning the city to its core. Although the buildings are concrete, Baltimore is in fact a jungle.

Naheem hadn't remembered it as quite this bad as a youth but children seldom realize just how unpleasant their environment really is until they gain some experience to measure it by. With this in mind, Naheem thought of the jungles number one rule, kill or be killed.

“Fuck it.” he reached for the remote to the TV.

Nasir slowly eased to the curb on 20th street and parked. 20th was a block over from North and Aisquith. Most of the block was abandoned. Nephew got out the truck with Hook and they walked a block over to the Quickie mart. Nephew saw a split between two dilapidated buildings and made a mental note.

When Nephew and Hook approached the Quickie Mart they saw a small crowd. Hook walked up in front of Nephew past the crowd and into the Quickie Mart. Nephew slowed down a bit scanning the crowd for Tavon. When he didn't see him he asked a short stocky light skin man in the crowd, “Yo... Who got the Haze out here?”

The man turned and face Nephew. Thinking that Nephew was harmless because of his age and his youthful face, he swiveled his neck and pointed to a silver Camaro on the far end of the parking lot.

“He over there sittin in the car.”

Nephew turned and strolled across the small parking lot and saw the heads of two people in the car. Hook came out the store and stood in place as he watched Nephew stalk his prey. Nephew approached the car from the front. Tavon sat in the passenger side of the car with a female on the driver side. They looked as if they were having a conversation. When Nephew got to the front of the car Tavon made an attempt to get out. He grabbed the door to push it open, Nephew pulled the Glock 19 from his waistband and shot through the front windshield. Tavon tried to duck down behind the dashboard and grab the.44 Bulldog he had under the seat.

The crowd in the parking lot disbursed except the man that directed Nephew to Tavon. He heard the first set of shots and made a move for his weapon. Hook was still in front of the store when the man reached in his waistband. Hook walked up behind him, put his .45 to the back of his head and flexed the trigger. The slug crashed in back of the man's head disfiguring his face upon it's exit. Hook was so close to his victim that the fire leaped from his .45 burning the hair around the entry wound.

Hook looked up and saw Nephew on the hood of the Camaro sending shots into its occupants. Nephew jumped off the hood of the car after the slide on the top of the Glock sat back indicating that he emptied the clip. Nephew jumped off the hood and took the lead running through the two buildings with Hook on his heels.

Tavon and Angie remained in the front seat of Angie's Camaro embracing each other's corpse with 21 shots split between them. When Nephew and Hook reached the truck they got in and Nasir slowly pulled away from the curb.

* * * * * * *

Twenty five minutes later they were back at the safe house telling Naheem about their successful mission. Hook was excited.

"You should've seen Nephew lil ass on top of the car givin that nigga the business! He look like me when I was young, almost brought tears to my eyes how sweet he looked."

"Oh yeah? Shorty showed his ass like that." Naheem

said smiling at Nephew.

“Man, I ain't even want to give it to that bitch like that. She started screamin loud as shit. I couldn't leave a witness.”

Naheem looked at Nephew and gave him the jungles doctrine. “Young Nephew, war only guarantees us one thing...”

“Casualties.” Nasir and Hook said completing Naheem’s sentence.

For the next hour they talked about the new roles that everybody would play then Naheem left and went home.

* * * * * * *

It was 8:37 when Naheem arrived home, he walked in the bedroom. Netta was sitting up on the bed wearing a T-shirt talking on the phone. She looked up at Naheem.

“Hey baby.”

Naheem bent over and kissed her on the forehead. Netta responded to the voice on the other end of the phone.

“Yeah, he just walked in.”

“Who's that bein all nosy?” Naheem playfully asked.

“It's April, she said hi.”

“I should've known. Tell Miss Bottoms I said what's up.”

Naheem walked into the bathroom and ran the water in the walk in shower. He sat in there for a moment. Netta could be heard out in the bedroom laughing on the phone. Naheem wondered just how happy she would be tomorrow when he popped the big question. The bathroom was now full of steam, Naheem undressed and got in the shower.

When he finished his shower he wrapped a towel around his waist, walked into the bedroom and over to the walk in closet. He dried off and put a pair of boxers on then reached to the overhead shelf and retrieved the backpack he left there. He dumped the money from the backpack to the carpet and counted out $15,000. Naheem could still hear Netta on the phone out in the bedroom. When the $15,000 was counted out he put it back in the backpack and put the rest in a grey Prada drawstring bag then went and joined Netta who was now off the phone and watching TV.

“Damn, what... My son don't like me no more.” Naheem joked about Princes absence.

"When I went over your grandmother's she said she was taking him to the circus tomorrow. He told me to tell his Da-Da that he was going to see monkeys and elephants so he need money. I gave your grandmother a hundred dollars for him.”

“Oh awight then. Sooo... he gon come home tomorrow night?”

“Yeah, she gonna call me when they get back.”

“So, umm... What you doin tomorrow?”

Netta thought for a second. “I got to meet the franchise lawyer at ten O’clock. His name is B. Fisher, I got his number off the internet and called. After that I'm not really doing anything, why?”

“I want you to meet me at the Harbor around six O’clock. I booked a boat ride from the Harbor to the Annapolis Harbor so we can have dinner at Philips. I already made the reservation.”

“That would be nice.” Netta laid her head on Naheem's bare chest.

“I know we ain't been out in a minute.” He said as he caressed her back and ran his fingers through her locks.

Naheem went on talking for another 15 minutes then he realized Netta had fallen asleep..

CHAPTER 10

The next morning Naheem awoke and reached across the bed to find the space where Netta should've been empty. All that was there was her warmth and fragrance. He got out of bed to relieve himself. Naheem heard the shower water running, he eased the bathroom door open to find Netta with her back to him washing herself. The soapy water running down the contours of her agile but firm body aroused him. He stepped into the shower with her, Netta felt his erection press against the small of her back. Naheem removed the soap from her neck and began kissing the back of Netta's neck and shoulders slowly working his way down her frame.

"Do we have time." She whispered.

Feeling her own heat rise Netta pressed her hands firmly against the wall for support as Naheem's tongue and mouth went to work allowing his actions to answer her question. He kissed the backs of her knees and she responded with a low moan.

"Mmmmm."

Naheem turned her around on her rubbery legs and

slowly began reversing his direction back up the front of her body. Netta gripped his shoulders as his tongue teasingly played on the inside of her thighs. Her pelvic moved forward involuntarily as his tongue flicked across her clitoris.

"Ahhh... Yesss."

As Naheem placed one of her legs across his shoulder, Netta grabbed hold of the shower head to keep from falling as his tongue worked her masterfully causing her juices to flow as climax after climax raked her body. Naheem held her up as her knees went limp.

Getting to his feet he lifted her up with his back on the wall and lowered her slowly onto his erection. Her face contorted and she bit down on her bottom lip as more of him entered her. Naheem looked in Netta's eyes as he slowly filled her. Netta nodded her head to let him know she wanted more. Not trusting her voice she continued to nod her head until she felt like Naheem had reached her stomach. Netta placed her hands on his shoulders, she used her upper body strength to move up and down on him to match his rhythm. Naheem began with slow long strokes until he felt the walls of Netta's love cave tighten around him and pull him in deeper. Feeling his own climax rising Naheem threw caution to the wind as he quickened his pace slamming every inch of himself into her. Netta held on tightly as her own orgasm shot through her body like electricity again and again. She moaned loudly as she felt Naheem pulsate and erupt within her.

"Oh… Shhhiit!"

Naheem slowly eased Netta to solid ground and slowly

washed her body allowing her trembles to subside and she returned the favor. Soon after, they got out the shower and got dressed. Naheem was in a bit of a rush because he had a full day ahead of him. After he was fully dressed he walked over to Netta who was in the walk in closet trying on shoes. Naheem pulled her close to him by her waist and kissed her passionately. When he went to break the embrace Netta didn't let go, she just stood there and held him tight with her head in his chest.

"I love you Naheem."

"I love you more Cupcake. Ima see you at six, call me when you get to the Harbor." Naheem said as Netta finally broke the embrace.

"Okay." She answered still really not wanting to let Naheem go.

At that moment Netta could've stood there and held him forever. She wondered if now was the time to tell Naheem that she was pregnant. She learned a week ago that she was eight weeks, she thought it would be better if she waited until tonight and broke the news to him over dinner. Naheem reached and grabbed the backpack from the overhead shelf, kissed Netta on the forehead and was out the door.

* * * * * * *

As Naheem made his way to the eastside of Baltimore he thought of the game and everything he had to leave behind with it. Today was officially his last day. As far as Naheem was concerned today was the mark of a new day, today is the day that he would kiss the game goodbye.

When Naheem reached the safe house he was greeted by Nasir, and Nephew. Nasir began to fill Naheem in on the changes that he made.

“I got Nephew hangin with us today so he’ll know how shit work. Tay-Tay in place ready to run Streeper and Ima run all the coke through Dinkles.”

Naheem nodded his head giving his consent of the positioning. Nasir lead the way to the lounge chair. A table loaded with money sat in front of it. Nephew sat on the arm of the chair while Naheem and Nasir took their seats. Nasir began by pointing to the larger pile on the table.

“That’s the $70,000 I owe.” Naheem didn’t move. Nasir continued, “That's 42 Nephew brought in. That pile right there is Dutch 14 and that's Tye’s 28. All together it's $154,000, Nephew counted everything behind me.” Nasir said.

Even though Nephew had counted the $154,000, to him it looked like a million dollars sitting on the table because it was all small bills. Naheem grabbed the $28,000 that came from Tye and gave it to Nasir.

“This all you.” Nasir pushed the $28,000 to the far end of the table.

“When I went to see Tye he told me his cousin Angie got hit last night.”

Naheem instantly put one and one together.

“Damn, that shit fucked up but I mean... what we supposed to do? What you tell him?”

“I told him just to keep his ear to the streets and to let me know if or when he hear anything. Shit... That's all I could tell him."

"Awight just stay on top of him." Naheem stood and started to put the rest of the money that was on the table in the backpack. Nasir took the $28,000 he'd just been given to the kitchen and placed it in a drawer.

Nephew spoke, "Yo, I ain't feelin' this."

Naheem turned to Nephew, "What?"

"Man, I crushed this nigga peoples and I got to do business with him too? I think the nigga need to go, who's to say that when I go to meet the nigga he don't bust my head?"

"I'll meet Tye myself." Nasir said walking out of the kitchen. "I don't see nothin getting back to him but if it do, I'll handle it."

"Awight." Nephew said dryly. Naheem went to the bathroom and returned with his Ruger in hand.

"You good Nephew?" He asked.

"Yeah I'm tight, I got rid of the dirty joint." Nephew affirmed.

"We gotta make moves." Naheem said while zipping the backpack.

* * * * * * *

Outside the apartment building Naheem threw the backpack in his trunk then got in Nasir's truck. As they rode Naheem's phone vibrated.

"Yeah."

"Nah, I just picked the ring up." Prinshe said.

"Awight, I got that paper for you too. I'll be there after I handle a few things."

"Okay."

When Naheem disconnected the call Nasir was turning into Lorelly. Once Nasir parked they got out and went into the building. In the apartment Naheem and Nasir took seats at the table and Nephew sat on the storage ben in the corner.

"Damn yo, ain't shit in here." Nephew announced as he looked around at the empty apartment.

"This where the donuts get made." Nasir said with a smile. "So what's up?" He asked Naheem.

"We just wait for now. Roberto said we'll know what's up today."

Naheem and Nasir briefed Nephew about the whole operation for 45 minutes then the doorbell rang. Naheem walked to the door and looked through the peephole. When he opened the door Gia stood there in full UPS uniform with a clip board in hand. She had a handcart with a Samsung TV box on it. Naheem went to reach for the clipboard when Gia spoke.

"Are you Mr. Branch?" She asked and winked her eye.

"Oh.. Ummm.. I'll get him for you." Naheem said. He turned to Nasir, "It's for you."

Nasir got up with an unsure look on his face. Naheem smiled and gestured to the door. When Nasir reached the door Gia said, "I have a package for a Mr. Branch."

"Yeah, that's me."

"Can you sign here sir." Gia pointed to an X on the paper. Nasir scribbled on the line next to the X.

"Thank you sir." Gia said as she pulled the handcart

from under the box. Nasir bent over and dragged the box into the apartment and closed the door.

“Touchdown.” Naheem said.

Nasir opened the box and brushed at the little white foam balls using his hand. He reached beneath the foam and pulled out a sixty pound compact square. The square was compressed so tightly that Nasir couldn't even rip the plastic off. Naheem told him, “You gon need a knife or razor.”

Nasir retrieved the mini box cutter that was on his keychain and made a small incision on the outer tape of the compact square, then he began to peel it off.

“Damn.” Nephew said as he saw the neatly stacked kilo's.

The kilos were also compressed, they were wrapped so tightly that the insignia of two AK 47's in the shape of an X could be seen through the plastic.

“Count’em, make sure your shit right.” Nasir heard Naheem say.

Nasir peeled all the plastic off the kilo's and counted 30 compact bricks in all. Because all the kilos were wrapped in the same plastic with the same insignia Nasir asked Naheem, “How we tell what's what.”

“We have to cut them open.” Naheem got up to assist Nasir.

Naheem took Nasir's box cutter and started cutting the plastic on the kilo's then handed them to Nasir to peel off.

“Nephew, look in the kitchen cabinet and get me that box of Ziploc bags.” Naheem kept his eye's on the drugs.

“Yo.. who was that mail lady?” Nasir asked with a bit of

caution. Naheem answered in a joking manner but meant every word.

“Oh her, she’s just one of the ones that's gon kill you if you fuck this money up.”

“She work for Roberto?” Nasir questioned.

“Yeah, that's Gia. That's his niece, she got a cousin name Kania that work for Roberto too, they the only two people he trust.” Naheem went in his pocket and gave Nasir the number that Roberto gave him. “When you text that number you ain't textin Roberto, you textin one of them and they get with him. He'll make the calls to get the order ready that's why it be takin two or three days sometimes.” Nephew returned with the box of Ziplocs and handed them to Naheem.

“Nephew I need you to put each joint in a Ziploc when Nasir pull the plastic off of them.” Nephew did as he was told and Naheem continued to brief Nasir.

“You see that address on the side of the box?”

“Yeah.”

“That's where you mail the money to. It won't never be the same address, I'll show you how to wrap the money and sent it. Whenever you get a shipment you always send the money back to the address that sent the package.”

“I ain't goin to no post office with a mill in a box, this ain't 85.” Nasir protested.

“Man dig this, this shit ain't just come from no post office. This shit came straight off a boat from Cuba some fuckin where to our front door. The money don't make it to the address. The address is just a tag so whoever Roberto got in the inside know which box to grab.” Naheem cut the plastic on the last kilo.

“Start looking for a new apartment to keep this shit in that only you and Nephew know about. You should be out of here by the end of the week.” Naheem instructed as he turned to Nephew.

“Nephew you can move in here when ya'll get the new spot but you got six months to move out further, you can’t stay in the hood no more shorty.”

“I can dig it.” Nephew said as he repackaged the kilo's. When all the kilos were repackaged Nasir showed Nephew how to cut the heroin.

“This shit ain't hard Nephew.”

“Naw, it ain't as hard as I thought it was.” Nephew admitted as he strained the scrambled heroin.

“Put enough in there so all the shops can have testers.” Naheem announced as he stood overlooking their progress.

“I got it.” Nasir said.

Naheem took the 29 kilo's and placed them in the kitchen cabinet while Nasir showed Nephew how to weigh the heroin they just cut and bag it. After the heroin was bagged Naheem pitched in and helped with the cleaning process.

“Nephew, I want you to take a ride with me real quick.” Naheem said as he wiped the table off. Nephew pushed the storage ben back up against the wall in the corner.

“Awight.” Naheem turned to Nasir who was in the kitchen washing his hands.

“I gotta make a run, take me to my car.”

“Awight, while you doin you Ima go ahead and make the drops.” Nasir said grabbing the three Ziploc bags of heroin. Once everything was bleached and wiped down they went out the door.

* * * * * * *

Nasir dropped Nephew and Naheem off at the top of the safe house parking lot and drove off. They walked through the parking lot to Naheem's car. As he took note of the bright sky, Naheem felt the warmth of the sun on his face. “Today is gon be perfect.” He thought. Naheem pressed the button on his key chain to unlock the car doors as they approached. He and Nephew climbed in and pulled off.

They rode in silence for a while as the sounds of Young Jeezy played. Every so often Naheem would look over at Nephew who was staring out the window mumbling Jeezy's lyrics. Naheem knew Nephew well, something was bothering him.

“What’s on your mind young nigga?” Naheem asked keeping his eye’s on the road.

“Ain’t shit.”

“It gotta be somethin. I know your young ass like the back of my hand. What it is?”

Nephew sat for a second searching for the right words to convey his thoughts.

“Man... I feel you movin on but I mean, I really can't explain it.”

“Yeah you can, Just say what is on your mind.”

Nephew turned his head to look out the window and took a deep breath. He turned to face Naheem.

“You all I got. My mother dead, my bitch ass father

could walk by me today or tomorrow and I wouldn't know who he was. I ain't got nobody, you the only family I got. I just feel like I'm getting left behind."

Naheem knew exactly how Nephew felt, he remembered vividly the day he was pushed out into the world alone. Just as he gathered the words to relay to Nephew he felt his phone vibrate.

"What's up?"

"Hey Naheem it's Sherry. I just left the courthouse with Kayo, he told me to tell you that the judge gave the State's Attorney a week to find the witness. He said if the State don't have his witness in seven days he gonna let Kayo go."

"Shit, that's what it is. If he call you, tell him to call me."

"Okay."

Naheem dropped the phone in his lap. As he turned onto Light Street, he parked and gave Nephew an account of what he was just told. They exited the vehicle, Naheem got the backpack out the trunk and they walked the short distance to Shay's Boutique.

The inside of the Boutique was busy as usual with the two floor workers tending to several customers at a time. Brittany was at the cash register ringing up shoes, she didn't even see Naheem until he spoke.

"What's up Brit, where shorty at?"

Brittany looked up for a second and saw Naheem and Nephew standing amongst the crowd.

"She in her office." She said as she worked the cash register.

Brittany reached under the counter and pressed a

button buzzing the door for them to go through. When they got to Prinshe's office, Naheem turned the knob to find that it was unlocked. They entered and found Prinshe behind her desk filling out paperwork.

"Heeey Nephewww." She said in a sing song voice that caused Nephew to blush.

"What's up Shay." He said still smiling.

Naheem sat on the huge desk placing the backpack beside him. Prinshe reached in the drawer of the desk and removed a little black drawstring bag that bore the logo of Black Pearl's Jewelry Galleria and handed it to Naheem. He reached in the bag and retrieved a black ring box. When Naheem opened the box the light danced on the diamond causing it to twinkle. He checked the inside of the band and saw that the engraved text was to his liking. Naheem closed the box and handed it to Nephew before he pushed the backpack in front of Prinshe.

"The fifteen got a red rubberband on it, I'll get the rest tomorrow."

Prinshe slid the backpack to the far end of the desk. Nephew handed the box back to Naheem and nodded signaling his approval. Naheem put the box in his pocket.

"You got everything set up?" Prinshe asked.

"Yeah, I think so. Ima go get a red velvet cake from Cake Diva's, she like their cakes. Ima take it to the yacht and make sure everything on their straight. She think we goin to eat at Philips in Annapolis. I gotta make moves, I got a few other things to handle before she meet me."

"Oh, alright. Just don't forget to call me."

"I got you." Naheem rose up off the desk.

"Bye Nephewww." Prinshe said in the same sing song voice and with a smile.

Nephew smiled back and waved as he and Naheem made their way out the door.

* * * * * * *

Reeva had been so devastated the past few days she could barely think straight. She being the only family Sean had in Baltimore meant that she was left to handle the funeral arrangements by herself. Reeva knew she had to be strong, not only for herself but for Sean as well. In her time of need she couldn't think of anybody she'd rather have at her side then Hook, and he being the gentleman he was he rushed to her aide. Just when Reeva thought bad couldn't get worst the mortician phoned her and told her that he couldn't reconstruct Sean's face. She and Hook drove to the funeral parlor to see what the mortician could do to avoid Sean having a closed casket funeral. The mortician explained that when the bullet exited the right side of Sean's face it left a gaping hole. So there was no other alternative but a closed casket. Reeva almost fainted as the mortician spoke. Hook wrapped his arms around her and lead her outside so she could get some fresh air.

Outside in the parking lot of Leroy Robert's Funeral Parlor, Hook leaned on Reeva's black BMW X5 as he held her while she cried to release some of the pain and frustration that the previous days had heaped upon her.

"Damn." Hook said to himself as a smoke grey Bentley Mulsanne pulled in the parking lot and stopped in front of them.

As Reeva lifted her head up off Hook's chest the Bentley's chauffeur got out and opened the back door. An attractive tall light skin man in a black tie and a black pin stripe suit stepped out on the lot.

"Re-Re." The man said. The chauffeur held the door for him. Reeva ran over to the man and gave him a hug. Hook just stood there wondering who the man could be.

"I guess this is Hook?" He asked Reeva after she broke their embrace.

Hook was already a little uneasy about not knowing who the man was but hearing him say his name made him paranoid. Reeva pulled the man by his hand over to where Hook was and introduced them.

"Uncle Jamar this is Hook, Hook this is my uncle Jamar." Jamar extended his hand to Hook. "Call me Chop's, all my friends call me Chop's."

Hook shook Jamar's hand. "Nice to meet you Mr. Chop's."

"My little Re-Re here has told me a lot about you. I appreciate you being the standup man you are."

Reeva cut in, "I told my uncle that you was a friend to Sean and how you've been looking out for me."

Hook jumped straight into his role. "Yeah Mr. Chop's, I do what I can you know? Your Nephew was a good dude, he was the type of guy that would give you anything."

"I see, my niece tells me that you and my Nephew had business arrangements that he's unable to continue for obvious reasons."

Hook didn't know what to say. He looked at Reeva who

was holding Jamar's hand as she smiled and nodded her head as if to reassure him.

“Yeah Mr. Chop’s... Me and Sean had our lil thing goin on.”

“Well Hook, with my Nephew gone I have two orders of business that must be taken care of immediately. First, I want a message sent to the fucks that did this to my Nephew and then I'm going to need someone to take my Nephew's place. My Re-Re tells me that you’re the man for both jobs.”

“What kind of message you want sent?”

“Come on Hook, it's no need to bullshit each other. I have $250,000 for you to find out who did this to my Nephew, that's more than enough for you to sprinkle around to see that my message is sent in an efficient manner. Once that's done, you can carry on where Sean left off.”

Hook smiled. “Well shit Mr. Chop’s, I'm sure I can get that message across any kinda way you want.”

Jamar rubbed his hands together and smiled, then he called his chauffeur who was standing by the Bentley's back door.

“Vincent... My bag please.”

Vincent moved to the trunk and retrieved a tan Coach men's gym bag and handed it to Jamar before he took his position by the back door of the Bentley.

Jamar received the Coach bag and handed it to Hook.

“This is $125,000 toward our new business venture, I'll give you the rest when the message is sent. I'm only in town for my Nephew’s funeral. I'll be flying out in seven days. While here, I'll be at the Ritz Carlton downtown. If you need me in the meantime my Re-Re can contact me."

"Ima see why I can't send that message while your still in town Mr. Chop's so we can jump start our new friendship." Jamar nodded his head and looked to Reeva who was holding onto Hook by his arm.

"Re-Re, I like this young man he should adjust well."

Reeva told Jamar about the mortician not being able to sew or staple Sean's face and that the end result of that was a closed casket. Jamar didn't speak he just listened to her update. Meanwhile Hook made a few brief calls, when he was done he asked Reeva to take him to his car. Jamar told Reeva that he would take her to Ruth's Chris later that night as she and Hook climbed into her truck. Vincent opened the door for Jamar as he approached and then everybodywenttheirseparateways.

CHAPTER 11

Driving west on North Ave., Naheem and Nephew rode in deep thought for a good eight or nine blocks. Finally at Charles Street Naheem broke the silence.

"You know Nephew... Your tongue and brain is the only tools that get sharper with use, you understand that?"

"I mean, I think so. You sayin the more you use your brain, the smarter you get."

"Right, that's exactly what I'm sayin. I learned a lot over the years and I grew out of a lot of shit too."

Nephew understood where Naheem was coming from and it made all the sense in the world to him yet he still felt abandoned. Nephew sat and listened as Naheem spoke although it took everything in him not to object.

"Ain't no love in this shit Nephew. We gotta use this shit while we can and get out. Ain't no loyalty, niggaz handshake's ain't matchin their smiles. Look at Livewire, the same niggaz he fed killed him. Better niggaz then me got fucked around in this game."

Nephew listened attentively and in his heart he knew

everything Naheem was saying was true.

“I feel where you comin from.”

Naheem stopped on Martin Luther King Blvd. directly in front of Cake Diva's. After he parked he told Nephew, “Ima be about five minutes.”

“I'll wait in the car then.” Nephew said as he pressed a button rotating the disc changer.

Naheem exited the vehicle and walked into Cake Diva's. The establishment was relatively small but was adorn with pastries of all sizes, shapes and colors encased in glass cubicles around the room. The sweet aroma of the goods along with the store’s stylish decor gave the establishment a warm and cozy feel. Naheem was greeted by an older pecan complexion woman with slightly gray hair and pretty white teeth in a white apron as he scanned the room admiring all the pretty items.

“Hi, can I help you with something?”

“Yes. Do you have any red velvet cakes?” Naheem inquired looking inside a showcase of desserts. The woman smiled.

“As a matter of fact I have one left.”

She then turned and walked in the back while Naheem waited patiently. From the huge bay window that was at the front of the store, Naheem could see Nephew getting out the car and walking toward the store as he spoke on the phone. Seconds later the woman returned with a tan box that she held with two hands and placed it on the counter top that separated her from Naheem.

“Fifty five fifty.” She said. A second later Nephew entered and joined Naheem.

"Man, I'm hungry as shit. That's all they got in here is cakes?"

"Yeah, that's it. We can go to Rusty Scupper in a minute."

Naheem paid the woman and Nephew gave him the car keys. They turned to leave with Nephew leading the way still on his phone. Naheem followed as he held the cake with two hands. Nephew pushed the door open just as the woman blurted out, "Your receipt sir!"

Naheem turned and saw his mother standing in the middle of the store wearing an white gown. The gown fluttered as if blown by a light breeze. The woman behind the counter was saying something with the receipt in her hand but he couldn't hear her. Naheem thought he was dreaming his mother just stood there almost as if she was hovering. Her eyes were as bright as he ever saw them, she looked at him and smiled. Nephew had just gotten the door all the way open for Naheem, he held it with his right hand as he used his left hand to dial on his phone.

"BOOOM!"

A gunshot rang out startling Naheem causing him to turn. He dropped the cake and grabbed his Ruger. Naheem saw Nephew's back arch inward as he fell toward the pavement. Naheem spun around the door with his weapon held high and saw a light skin man with freckles wearing a pair of Rayban Aviator sunglasses and a dark blue windbreaker with the letters D.E.A. written in yellow on the front. His Sig Sauer was pointed down aiming at Nephew as he advanced from a few feet away. Naheem released three shots with precision, all of which landed in different parts of the man's chest stopping him in his tracks. Naheem bent over to lift Nephew up and into the car when he saw a blood stain surrounding a hole in his shirt on the top left side of his back.

"Come on nigga... Get the fuck up!"

Once on his back Naheem saw another hole and blood stain on the right side of Nephew's chest. His eyes were glassy as he stared up at Naheem's eyes.

"I got you shorty."

Just as Naheem got to his feet with Nephew in his arms more shots rang out.

He felt a burning sensation from a projectile that ricocheted off a light pole and hit him in his left calf causing him to loose balance. Naheem dropped Nephew and fell on top of him hard. His chest hit Nephew's compact 40 cal. Naheem took the compact 40 out of Nephew's waistband and laid on top of him while he tried to locate the direction of the shooter. The sound of gravel made Naheem peek under his car and see the feet of someone tipping toward the rear. Naheem pushed himself to his feet catching his pursuer off guard. He leaned on the driver side of his car extending both hands over its roof, that's when he noticed the other gunman wearing a D.E.A. jacket also. Naheem squeezed the triggers. The first shot from the Ruger pushed the man back but he quickly regained his balance as he pivoted and tried to up his Sig Sauer. Naheem let the compact 40 rip twice with supreme accuracy hitting the assassin in his chest. Slug number three found its way to the man's forehead blowing chunks of his brains out the back of his head. Nephew could be heard moaning in pain behind Naheem. As Naheem turned, a single shot came through the passenger window to the driver side window hitting him in the abdomen and knocking him backward a few steps until he stumbled over Nephew.

"Fuck." Naheem cried out in agony as he fell and hit the back of his head on the pavement causing him to briefly see stars.

The shots came one behind another as Naheem fought to get up. Stray bullets whizzed by his head. The shop's huge bay window shattered sending pieces of glass everywhere as the bullets kept coming. Naheem tried to crawl back to the side of his car. He slid over Nephew and spotted a lone tear that ran out his right eye down the side of his face. Nephew stared up at Naheem as he took one last breath and released his grip on life.

Nephew's young body fought as long as it could. A bullet had grazed his heart causing severe damage. Naheem could tell by the blank gaze in his eyes that he was dead. Furious, Naheem's fear turned into blind rage. Even as bullets continued to whiz overhead he sprang to his feet. His would be executioner on the other side of the street was also wearing a D.E.A. jacket. Holding his breath, Naheem balled up his face and squeezed the triggers on the Ruger and 40 cal. displaying an expertise in marksmanship from all the practice he had gotten in the streets.

Spent shells leaped from his guns as he continuously pulled the triggers. Now on the defensive, the D.E.A. gunman bent his head low and dove on the ground. Wailing sirens could be heard in the distance as the gunfight progressed. The slide on the compact 40 sat back indicating that it was empty. Naheem continued to exchange fire with his foe as he placed the 40 in his pocket.

As he removed his hand from his pocket he tried to place his free hand on the Ruger for more accuracy when he felt his arm jerk. Naheem's adrenaline pumped pure anger causing him not to feel the shot to his left bicep. He held his Ruger up and continued to trade rounds. The sirens were getting closer by the minute. Naheem heard the roaring of an engine, then saw a cranberry colored H2 Hummer with dark tint abruptly stop in the middle of the street between he and his assailant as the slide on the Ruger sat back. The gunman jumped in the Hummer and it peeled off.

The shootout had lasted only 3 minutes but to Naheem it seemed like 3 hours as he fought for his life. Hobbling to his bullet riddled car, his hand smeared the door handle with blood as he opened it and slid in then placed the Ruger on his lap. He put the key into the ignition, fired the engine and burned rubber leaving the carnage behind. As he escaped, he took one last look at Nephew lying out on the sidewalk. Nephew looked as innocent as he did the day he entered the world.

Naheem made a quick U-turn in the middle of the street, the tires screeched as he made his way toward the Interstate. Once there he moved with the pace of traffic. He reached on his lap and threw the Ruger out the window over the Interstate and into the water below then repeated the same course of action with Nephew’s compact 40. Naheem saw police and ambulance on the other side of the

Interstate 83 going the opposite way rushing to the scene. He shook his head and bang the steering wheel in a fit of frustration. As he increased speed, the wind swept through the car. He turned the radio up to drown the sounds of the loud breeze...

Lord know I know,
I feel like can't nobody fuck with me,
And God got my back so,
Boosie keep his mind at ease,

Lil Boosie's powerful lyrics followed by the heavy 808's and intricate drum patterns reared through the Bose speakers as Naheem maneuvered in and out of the flow of traffic at 88 mph on Interstate 395. Fighting to keep his eyes open, Naheem was determined to live as he tried to regulate his breathing. He was hit pretty bad. His injuries included a shot to the left bicep and one to the left calf muscle, both of which were in and out wounds. He was more concerned with the wound in his abdomen, which he held with his left hand. As he removed his hand from the burning wound in his gut he noticed that he was bleeding profusely.

As Naheem passed the Raven's M&T stadium he glanced at his almost useless blood drenched hand and at that very moment he felt a chill over his body although beads of perspiration burst through his pores like a linebacker through an offensive line. Naheem shifted his gaze from his hand back to the wound in his stomach. The hole was no bigger than that of a pencil. The bottom half of Naheem's white Affliction shirt was dark red. Placing his hand back over the wound Naheem thought out loud and shook his head from side to side.

"Shit! Bitch ass niggaz got me good."

Visions of Netta and Prince quickly flooded him, forcing him into overdrive. At the thought of possibly dying and leaving his son another tear managed to escape his right eye.

"Gotta get to the hospital."

Feeling his heavy eyelids attempting to close, Naheem snapped back to reality and willed himself to stay alert. On the lookout for the police, every so often he peered up into his rearview mirror to scan the traffic behind him. Finally, after weaving around several cars to get ahead, he pressed his foot all the way down on the gas pedal and the car shot up to 110 mph and pinned him back against his seat.

Bearing to the right on the Hanover Street exit, Naheem decided it would be best if he slowed down to a moderate speed to approach the light. After crossing the Hanover Street bridge Naheem thought, "Damn, the hospital only up the street."

The hospital that he had in mind was Harbor Hospital which was now approximately three hundred yards ahead. Naheem was ten feet from the last light he had to go through to make the left in the hospitals parking lot when he lost consciousness and went through the red light. The huge loss of blood sent Naheem into shock causing him to lose consciousness again. His state of comatose was so deep that as he rolled through the red light he wasn't even awaken when a speeding F-150 rammed into the passenger side of his car in the middle of the intersection spinning it over forty five degrees. The car veered off to the left and came down on all four wheels when it hit the curb. With the hospital only a hundred yards ahead Naheem lay slumped in his car motionless dangling helplessly between life and death.

The airbags in the F-150 exploded on impact temporarily knocking the woman and her girlfriend out. The two young women awoke moments later to several pedestrians trying to pry their doors open. Due to impact, both doors were jammed. The young ladies climbed out the driver side window. With tears in her eyes and her right hand over her mouth the driver managed to say, "OO-MMY- GAWD!"

She saw the horrific sight of a man laid on the sidewalk with so much blood on him nobody could place it's source. The man lay on little pieces of broken windshield glass that the sun reflected off causing the street and sidewalk to look as if diamonds had grown from the concrete. The F-150's driver broke down into heavy sobs while her girlfriend held her in a comforting manner. Her sobs were so loud that she didn't hear the spectator that tried to take Naheem's pulse.

"You can stick a fork in this one baby, he done."

The passenger of the F-150 comforted her girlfriend as tears rolled silently down her face.

To Be Continued....

AN EXCERPT FROM CONCRETE JUNGLE II

Today was a bright beautiful day in the city of Baltimore. Hook leaned on a picnic table under a gazebo in the middle of Patterson Park with a MCM backpack on his chest, his brand new YZ 450 was leaning on its kickstand on the other side of the table from where he was, kids played on the playground a few feet away laughing and enjoying the summer's day. Hook took note of a man to the left of him out in the distance throwing a tennis ball for his grizzly bear size rottweiler to retrieve. He was all smiles when he saw a black Honda Coupe approaching from the other side of the park. The Honda came to a stop in front of the gazebo where Hook now stood. The door opened and the occupant spoke as he got out.

"What's good bro?" Hook walked towards him and gave him some dap.

"Everything good my nigga, that's what we here for ain't it?'

"Damn bro, whats up with the bag?"

Hook looked down at the backpack without saying a word and unzipped it displaying the rubber banded stacks of money inside.

"This is the coins for the job."

“Bro, word on the street is whoever Naheem was copping from set him up but ya'll been fucking the streets up.”

“Yeah man shit crazy, that’s why I need you. I know I can count on you to get the job done and over with, I got $50,000 for you to handle this last issue.”

The man fell silent for a moment before Hook continued. “I got all the info you gonna need when I hit your phone with dude location and description just come through.”

“Fuck it, I'm in I can't turn down that kind of paper.”

In between the negotiation one of the kids from the playground could be seen walking in their direction.

“You know I'm all about my paper Broski?!”

“I'm hip, that’s why you the man for the job.”

Hook took the backpack off and placed it on the green picnic table when the kid walked up to the dirt bike.

“Is this your bike?” He asked as he eyed the huge bike. Hook didn’t have a chance to answer.

“Fuck on away from here lil nigga, you nosey as shit!” The little boy was startled by the man's sudden aggression.

Hook didn't bother to say a word, he just took a rubber banded stack out the bag and handed it to the man, then placed the backpack back on his chest.

“Damn bro, this kinda light.”

“My fault bro, it do look a little light.”

Hook was given the stack of money back and placed it on the picnic table then he thumbed through the stacks in the backpack.

The man turned and was about to scold the kid again for

touching the bike when Hook interrupted.

“Yo, don't get that on the bike.”

“Don't get what?”

The man was cut off in midsentence as he stared into the Glock that Hook retrieved from the backpack.

“Sorry Brodie but Ima need those keys.”

“Man you trippin I thought we was good.”

“We is.” Hook said in a matter of fact tone.

Just then the kid calmly walked around the table and dug in the man's pockets in search of the keys.

“Hook man, what the fuck is this?!”

“Damn yo, you a contract killa and you cryin like a bitch. You know what the fuck it is.”

Hook jerked the trigger of his Glock twice sending the man’s brains all over the far end of the table. The kid grabbed the $5000 that Hook left on the table before the man’s body hit the ground and ran toward the Honda coupe. Hook stuffed his Glock back in the backpack and jumped on his dirt bike kicking it to life, then he yelled over his shoulder.

“Yo, follow me and keep up!”

The kid didn’t bother responding he just turned the radio up and the lyric's from Uncle Murda blared in the air.

Niggaz get shot everyday B
You be aight
You tough right
Camron voice

* * * * * * *

“How many miles this bitch got,” Ricco asked as he

circled a white Audi Q7.

“43k but she's fully loaded with the Bison Body kit and those is Asanti rims.”

“That ain't bad, what’s the tag?”

“For you... $44,995.”

Ricco threw the car salesman a brown paper bag across the hood of the trunk then said, “That’s $30,000 I'll bring you the rest next month”.

“You know the rules Ricco, I'll do the paperwork up like your making monthly payments. The tags gotta stay on until your done paying the truck off, you got six months to complete the cash payments.”

“Damn nigga, I just told you I was gonna bring you the rest next month. I bought my last 4 cars from here,” Ricco said with a bit of an attitude but he knew he had to hold his composure because Diamond Motors was the only place where you could go in the city that would allow people to pay any cash amount for any vehicle and making it appear that they was making payments. This caused this particular lot to be a hot spot for hustler's all over the city.

“I understand Ricco but I have to do my job and explaining the rules to you before every purchase is my job. Now... I'll run this through the machine and start the paperwork. I'll be back out with the keys in 10 minutes,” the salesman retorted.

As the salesman turned to go into the trailer, Ricco mumbled under his breath, “Bitch ass nigga.”

Ricco then called his girlfriend Sky who had dropped him off at the lot twenty minutes before.

“Hey Bae, did you see anything you like,” she said in

her normal upbeat tone.

"Yeah… Ima get this little Audi truck, it's nice. Don't think you gonna be driving my shit all the time either."

"I don't wanna drive your funky truck boy. I'll just wait until my birthday which is only a month and a half away, so you can upgrade me."

"I ain't forget, you want the M4 drop."

"I did, but I want a Panamera now, they sooo cute."

"A what… your pussy ain't like that!"

"It might not be, but this ass and head pick up the slack! I got Wraith head and Maybach ass."

"That you do, but we gonna take that Wraith head and Maybach ass to the auction to get a M4." Ricco said through a laugh then continued, "I'll be done here in a couple minutes, meet me at the house in about twenty and we gonna slide out Tyson's."

The conversation lasted only a few minutes more before Ricco spotted the salesman emerging from the trailer. He ended the call and leaned on his new truck awaiting the key's.

"All done Ricco, I hope you enjoy your new truck," the salesman said with a shy grin as he lightly pitched the keys.

"So we good?"

"Absolutely… until next month that is."

Ricco was too happy about his current purchase to enter into a war of words so he got in the truck not bothering to say anything. He brought the truck to life and quickly pulled out missing the salesman by a few inches. He stopped at the entrance of the lot to adjust the rearview mirror only to see the salesman wiping himself of dust.

Ricco chuckled and made a right turn, he admired the way the dual pipes purred as he increased speed. He was in the middle lane approaching a red light when a dark green Dodge Ram pickup switched lanes cutting him off.

"Stupid ass nigga!" He cursed as if the motorist could hear him.

Ricco sat at the red light and adjusted his side mirrors. He used the view of the Denali behind him to align the mirror's to his liking. When he was done, he reached over in the passenger seat where he had thrown his phone when his truck rocked like he'd been bumped.

Ricco looked back, the Denali had pushed him into the rear of the Dodge pickup wedging him in between the two. He tried to open the driver side door when he saw a masked man rapidly approaching from the back. He then tried to crawl over to the passenger side door when he saw another masked man from out the back window trotting, then stop at the back door of the truck. That's when he heard the shots.

The AR-15 and SK sounded off, the discharged bullets knocked all the windows out and left gaping holes in the truck.

The man wielding the AR took his time as he slowly walked along side of the truck casually spraying. Ricco curled up under the steering wheel in an useless attempt to hide. He was hit or grazed by bullets or fragments everywhere but the bottom of his feet at this point. The AR ceased fire and the man with the SK briskly walked up to the driver side window. He stuck the SK in the window and pointed it at Ricco under the steering column squeezing the trigger at point blank range. The force of the bullet's slamming into Ricco felt like trucks hitting him from every angle.

The little thread of life that Ricco was holding on to had just been cut short. Blood covered the front interior of the truck. Bits and pieces of Ricco were everywhere from the driver side to the passenger side. The Dodge pickup peeled off through the white smoke left in the air from the tactical assault weapons. The two assassin's calmly walked back to the Denali stepping on spent shell casings as they made their escape. The Denali backed up off the trucks bumper then swerved around the Audi in the opposite direction of the Dodge Ram.

* * * * * * *

Lil Dee followed Hook to Eager Street. Small garage's lined both sides of the street. When they got to the middle of the block Hook stopped in front of a garage that served as a make shift mechanic shop. Hook waved Lil Dee into the garage as he pulled in. An older man with a salt and pepper color beard and a baldhead appeared from the garage next door. He was wearing a brown one piece jumpsuit that was heavily stained with grease and oil. He wiped his hands on an oil soaked rag before he spoke.

"Is this it?"

"Yeah this is it Uncle Wilbur." Hook said as he dismounted the bike.

"What's up pop's?"

"Hey Darius," Wibur said. He then snapped his fingers

as if he'd just remembered something. “What happen to those stones you said you was gonna give me?”

“This is the stones right here.” Lil Dee said as he pointed to the car with a smile.

“Come on with the dumb shit Darius, you said you had some ready for me!”

“Man fuck you, you think you pressin me or something?” Lil Dee fumed as he gripped the .380 on his hip.

Hook quickly spoke up, knowing Lil Dee wouldn’t think twice about killing his own father.

“Naw Unc, we giving you the car to do whatever you wanna do with it. Flip it or sell the parts, it don't matter keep the money.”

Wilbur perked up as Hook spoke, all he thought about was how much crack he would be able to purchase with the proceeds. It didn’t matter that his son was seconds from murdering him in cold blood, he wiped sweat from his brow and smiled, displaying a huge gap in his mouth where his two front teeth use to be.

“I'm done fixing your bike Darius, its next door.”

Lil Dee didn’t answer, he just walked to the garage next door. He came back out in a matter of seconds pushing a lime green and black KX 85.

“What that shit sound like Dee?”

Lil Dee scooted onto the bike and kicked it to life. Hook nodded his approval at the way the bike sounded. Lil Dee lightly jerked the throttle back and forth as he listened to the bike scream.

“You like that, huh Darius?”

Lil Dee revved the bike louder as he ignored his father. After he was satisfied with the work that Wilbur had done he turned the bike off. In that instant he heard a couple of other bikes.

It sounded like they were headed in their direction and fast. Hook looked at Lil Dee and simultaneously they retrieved their weapon's holding them down by their legs as they scanned both ends of the tiny block.

A Husqvarna 450 and CRF 450 turned into the block. When Hook and Lil Dee saw them they both smiled anticipating the upcoming show. Lil Net rode the Husqvarna as if his life depended on it. He stood as he rode the huge bike holding it up at almost a full 12 o'clock with his left foot on the seat and his right leg kicked out behind him. From a distance it appeared that he was trying to pull the bike down by the way he rocked back and forth. Lil Dev rode alongside of Net with the CRF at a full 12 o'clock wheelie with his right leg crossed over the left.

The two young stuntmen stopped in front of Lil Dee. By this time both Lil Dee and Hook had concealed their weapon's. Lil Dee was kind of disappointed, he was hoping for a little action. A shootout would've made his day right now but the sight of his two friends made him feel better than any gun fight would.

"Ya'll niggas is fast, we saw Hook getting it across Monument Street. By the time we got to the bikes in the alley you was gone and I couldn't hear the bike no more so we ain't know where you went," Lil Dev said to Hook. "We just took a guess coming around here."

Net cut in focusing his attention in on Wilbur. "Aye Ill

Will, What's up with that bread you owe me?"

Everybody turned to look at Wilbur as Net inquired about the money he owed. Hook didn't give Wilbur a chance to answer, he turned to Net and asked him. "What he owe you?"

"He came and got an eight ball from me four days ago. That shit ain't nothin foreal."

"Damn Net, I fix all your bikes and all Dev bike's for next to nothin." Wilbur said in an attempt to defend himself.

Lil Dee was looking at the ground shaking his head in shame when Hook said, "Dee pay him."

"What? Pay who? For what? I might not!"

Net and Dev laughed at Lil Dee's dramatics but Hook didn't find anything funny. He looked at Lil Dee and the fire in his eyes could be seen as he spoke through clinched teeth.

"Give him the money!"

"Hook man, I ain't smoke no coke. Plus, he got this car we just gave him."

"Pay...him...now!"

Lil Dee mumbled under his breath as he went in his pocket. He pulled the stack of bills out of his pocket.

"Naw man, that shit ain't nothin. I'll just bring everybody in the hood bike around here. Ill Will can work it off. I'll race you for five hundred though."

"Damn...you must ain't really want the money. You just givin money away today, who you think you is Bea Gaddy?" Lil Dee said as he shoved the money back in his pocket before continuing. "you a stunt man Ima rider!"

Wilbur hadn't lost sight of his goal, he had to speak up now before Lil Dee got away. Soon as everything was ironed out Wilbur cleared his throat. "Darius...um, can I holla at you real quick?"

"What's up yo?" Lil Dee snapped.

"Being as though I got this car I was wondering that if...I mean when I get the money off it could you sell me an ounce?"

Lil Dee couldn't believe what he'd just heard. He looked from Wilbur to Hook who just smiled and shrugged his shoulders, back to Wilbur again. He sucked in a lung full of air and blew it out.

"Yeah yo, C.O.D."

"Thanks man. I lov---"

Wilbur was cut off in midsentence by Lil Dee kicking the bike back to life and revving the engine. Lil Net and Lil Dev followed suit. Dev pointed to Dee for him to lead the pack, he shot up the street with Dev and Net on the trail. Hook pushed his bike in the garage where Lil Dee's bike had been. When he came out Wilbur had a blank look on his face.

COMING SOON!!!
FOLLOW MEDIA44 ON OUR FACEBOOK AND INSTAGRAM

Order Form

MAKE CHECKS AND MONEY ORDERS PAYABLE TO:

Shawnita Fenwick
P.O. BOX 24651
Baltimore, MD 21214

Name:____

Address:______________________________________

City:______________ State:_____________

Zip:______________

Amount		Book Title or Pen Pal Number	Price
		Included for shipping for 1 book	**$4 U.S. / $9 Inter**

This book can also be purchased on:
AMAZON.COM/ BARNES&NOBLE.COM/ CREATESPACE.COM

Made in the USA
Columbia, SC
24 November 2024

47490028R00085